HARDER BETRAYAL

LESSER
BOOK 3

PENELOPE SKY

HARTWICK PUBLISHING

Hartwick Publishing

Harder Betrayal

CONTENTS

1. Elise   1
2. Grave   9
3. Camille   17
4. Cauldron   23
5. Elise   29
6. Grave   47
7. Camille   59
8. Elise   69
9. Camille   79
10. Grave   97
11. Camille   105
12. Elise   117
13. Cauldron   125
14. Camille   131
15. Cauldron   145
16. Camille   149
17. Cauldron   167
18. Elise   191
19. Grave   205
20. Cauldron   213
21. Camille   231
22. Camille   243
23. Cauldron   259
24. Camille   277
25. Grave   287
26. Cauldron   297
27. Camille   303

28. Elise   319

29. Grave   327

30. Cauldron   339

31. Elise   351

32. Camille   363

33. Grave   385

34. Camille   393

Epilogue   399

1

ELISE

When I walked in the door, I almost didn't recognize him.

His plump face was black and purple, and there were dried cuts on his skin. His nose looked out of place, like someone had cracked the bone and pushed it to the left.

He turned in his chair to regard me. "It's as bad as it looks."

I took the seat beside him and let my eyes roam over his face. "Did Kyle do this to you...?"

He gave a sigh. "I warned you."

"Jerome, I'm so sorry..." At the end of the day, I had rights. If I didn't want to sleep with someone, I didn't have to. This type of retribution was totally unnecessary.

"Grave is paying us extra, so I guess that makes it worth it." He grabbed the envelope and handed it to me.

I let it hang in the air between us, too guilty to take it. "You think that's the end of Kyle?"

"I don't know," he said with a sigh. "There's not much left to say."

I took the envelope of cash and stuffed it into my pocket.

"He'll get over it eventually. The second he sees some other hot thang, he'll forget all about you."

"I hope so."

"So, what is it with Grave?"

"What do you mean?"

"Is this the beginning of your retirement?"

I held his gaze while I experienced all those flashbacks. "I'm not sure. All I know is, I don't want to fuck another client when I already have a client I like. Get paid to do what you love, and you never work again, right?"

"What's different about Grave than the other ones? He's a good-looking guy, but he's not the only one."

"I don't know... Not sure I can explain it."

Jerome studied me for a while. "Well, let me know when you're ready for another client. For now, I'll just keep collecting the payments."

I had just stepped outside when I came face-to-face with the man I didn't want to see.

In a three-piece suit with the glint of arrogance in his eyes, he didn't seem surprised to see me. As if one of his men had informed him of my arrival at the bar so he could run down here to face me.

I knew this encounter was inevitable, so I held my stance and faced him with a straight spine.

His eyes swept across my face as he took in my appearance. "I'm sorry about Jerome."

"No, you aren't." I stepped around and moved to the street where a car was waiting.

Of course, he chased after me. "We had a deal, Elise."

"Deals come and go. Get over it." I opened the back door.

He slammed his hand on the door and forced it shut. He crowded into me, coming so close his body nearly touched mine. "I'll pay double his rate."

"It's not about the money, Kyle."

"Then what is it about? He's good in bed? Give me a try."

"Get your fucking hand off the door."

He leaned his entire body up against it instead. "Elise, come on."

"Just let it go. I'm not the only beautiful woman on the market."

"But you're the most beautiful—and don't pretend you don't know that."

I narrowed my eyes in annoyance. "I'm not worth this crusade, Kyle. I think you just want what you can't have—and that's very childish." I shoved him hard in the chest so I could free up the back door. "Now leave me the fuck alone."

I pulled up outside Grave's building. *Can I come up?*

You don't need to ask, sweetheart.

My altercation with Kyle melted off my body the second I read that. I entered his building then took the elevator to the top floor. When the doors opened and I entered the parlor, Grave was already there waiting for me. It was late in the evening, so he was in nothing but his low-rise sweatpants, his powerful chest a living slab of concrete.

I thought I'd never see this place again.

I hung my coat on the rack, one of the pockets stuffed with the envelope of cash. Then I turned into him, surrounded by his warmth immediately. My cheek rested against the hardest pillow I'd ever felt, and I sank into it.

Big arms surrounded me and pulled me close, his lips resting on the top of my head.

I could stay like that forever.

He held me like that for nearly a minute before he pulled away. "Hungry?"

"No."

"Thirsty?"

"No."

He stared down at me for a few seconds, and then that playful smirk emerged. "Straight down to business, then."

My arm hooked through his, and we headed to his bedroom. The fire in the hearth had already heated the room, casting shadows along the walls, and filling the room with popping noises that made me think of camping as a kid.

With his back turned to me, he dropped his sweatpants and his boxers, showing his muscular ass before he walked to the bed. He got on top, leaned against the pile of pillows at the headboard, and stretched out his arms across the bed. "Get to it."

I slowly undressed, taking my time dropping every piece of clothing. With each article that hit the floor, he got that much harder, twitching occasionally. With unblinking eyes, he stared at me until I was buck naked, the glow of the fire noticeable against my skin. No man had ever made me feel sexier than he did. All he did was give me a look, and every insecurity I had was washed away.

I climbed onto his big bed and made my way up his chest, like a wildcat climbing up a tree. My knees parted and straddled his hips, and I sat right on his length, my sex already smearing against his bare skin.

I could tell he felt it because he took a quiet breath.

My hands planted on his chest, and I arched my back so I could drag my body down and scoop him into me. On the first try, I succeeded, getting the head of his dick right at my entrance, too thick to fit without some grinding.

Slowly, we came together, my wetness smoothing his entrance.

Then we were reunited, as if it'd been weeks since we'd been together rather than days.

Like a bear that woke from hibernation, he grabbed my hips with his big hands and dragged me down, sealing me over his entire length.

It hurt. But it hurt good.

His hands traveled to my ass and squeezed the cheeks before he let me rise again. "Worth every penny."

2

GRAVE

I lay in bed with her in my arms, staring at the fireplace as my mind drifted. I had a lot of shit on my plate and nowhere to start, and I certainly couldn't start now, not with Elise on my chest. A part of me wondered if I should just kill Kyle to make my life easier. A little hunch told me his story wasn't over.

A light knock sounded on the bedroom door.

My eyes immediately flicked to it, my chest suddenly stagnant as my breath died in my lungs.

The knock sounded again, this time a little louder.

My butler would never bother me in the middle of the night like this—unless it was important.

Like life-and-death important.

I did my best to roll Elise over without waking her. Her eyes opened briefly, and she gave me a look of daggers for disturbing her. But she seemed to nod off again immediately, hugging a pillow instead of me.

I slipped on my sweatpants before I stepped into the hallway. "What is it?" I asked the question before the door was fully closed.

"Camille is here to see you."

It took a solid two seconds to process what he'd said. "Why?"

"I don't know, sir."

"It's almost midnight."

"She just said she needed to see you." He dismissed himself and walked away.

I watched him go, my mind immediately jumping to my brother's well-being. I entered the parlor a moment later, finding her sitting on one of the couches, her arms and legs close to her body as if fighting to stay warm. When I entered the room, she looked up at me with her green eyes.

I stared back. She'd been the woman in my life for years, and I could still read her like words on a page. I stepped into the seating area, taking the nearby armchair. "What's happened?"

She didn't speak.

"Tell me my brother lives."

She gave a slight nod. "Cauldron's fine. A lot better than I am, actually…"

My eyes shifted back and forth as I stared into her face, seeing the bloodshot eyes, the bags of skin that hung underneath them, the grayish color of her once brilliant complexion. She'd somehow aged fifteen years since I last saw her.

"He dumped me." The words were so quiet I could barely hear them. Her eyes were down, either ashamed or wounded. "Just like that…"

I didn't know what to say.

"The second he came home from Paris. As if he couldn't get the words out fast enough."

"He didn't seem different to me."

"Well, you weren't stupid enough to tell him you love him." She crossed her arms tighter over her chest. "It slipped out when we were having dinner. I didn't even say it to him directly, just said it in passing, but that was enough to…to make him run."

"What was his reason?"

"That someday I would get hurt...the way his mother did. At first, I thought his reason was sweet...until he said the next thing."

"And what was that?"

Her lips started to quiver, and the dam behind her eyes began to crumble. "That he wouldn't walk away from his work to be with me...that I'm not enough of a reason." She gave a loud sniff then steadied herself, locking her cries inside an invisible cage. "What did he say when you spoke to him?"

"He didn't mention you at all."

She gave a slight nod. "What did you talk about?"

"Roan."

"And that's it?"

"We spoke of Elise as well. She asked me to be her full-time client."

That information seemed to mean something to her because she closed her eyes briefly and let out a sigh. "This is the part where you get to relish your victory. You get to say I told you so. You get to tell me how fucking stupid I am..."

I didn't say a word.

The silence lingered until she raised her chin to look at me.

"I'm sorry."

Her eyes watered, like that response was far more painful.

"I'll talk to him."

"Don't."

"I know how to—"

"I said *don't*. Wouldn't take him back even if he called me right now and asked me to come home. I mean...to his home." She looked away again. "He's hurt me too many times. I'm done giving him chances." She gave another sniff, her eyes wet, her nose runny.

"Then why are you here?"

Silence. Long silence. "After I left Cap-Ferrat, I drove straight here. It was a long drive, and when I got to Paris, I didn't know where else to go. I have to start over now, and I don't even know how."

"You can sleep here and worry about that in the morning." I didn't owe Camille anything, not when I already gave her everything. But I wouldn't turn her away, not in the middle of the night, not when she was delirious in her sorrow. And I wouldn't turn her away for my brother—because I knew he cared for her.

"That's really nice of you." She started to cry.

I reached my hand toward her arm, to give her the kind of affection that would make her feel less alone. Though my hand hovered there and never made contact. It was close enough that I could even feel the warmth of her skin. But then I pulled away and returned my hand to my knee.

She didn't see it. "Despite everything he did and said, I know he cares about you."

She released a scoff and a laugh mixed together. "Right."

"I know he'll thank me."

"He won't because you aren't going to mention this to him." She raised her chin and looked at me. "I kept my shit together until I was gone, and I don't want him to know how much he's destroyed me."

I held her gaze.

"Please don't tell him."

"I can't lie to my brother, Camille."

"Please." She pleaded with me with desperate eyes.

"I won't go out of my way to mention it to him. But if he brings it up, I will."

Her eyes moved past my shoulder, looking behind me.

I heard Elise's quiet footsteps grow louder as she approached. I turned to look at her, wishing she hadn't woken up.

"Is everything okay?" she asked, wearing one of my shirts that fit her like a dress. Her hair was a mess and so was her makeup, but through all of that, you could see the genuine concern.

Camille seemed paralyzed with embarrassment. "I'm so sorry. I didn't realize you had company."

I always had company.

"I didn't mean to wake you," Camille said.

Instead of taking the seat beside me, Elise moved to my lap, her arm hooking around my shoulders. "You didn't." She turned to give me a look, a look that said my absence was the cause of her disturbance.

Camille quickly wiped her eyes with her fingertips. "It's late... I should get to bed." She left the couch and moved into the other room, looking for my butler to help her set up for the evening.

Elise and I returned to the bedroom, the fireplace cold. My lamp on the nightstand was on, so it wasn't pitch black. I removed my bottoms and got back into bed as if nothing had happened.

Elise joined me, still in my t-shirt. "Did something happen with her and Cauldron?"

"He ended things."

"Why?" she asked, surprised.

"To protect her, I guess."

"Protect her from what?"

I gave a shrug. "It was just an excuse."

"Then what is the real reason?"

I turned on my side and spooned her from behind. "Because he's incapable of loving anyone."

3

CAMILLE

I'd wound up at Grave's apartment because I didn't know where else to go. When I left Cap-Ferrat, I headed to Paris because that was where I'd spent my entire life. But once I got there, I didn't know what to do next. My car was loaded with all my possessions, and I didn't want to move all of it into a hotel or leave it in the car. It was the middle of the night, and I wouldn't find a new apartment at that hour. Besides, I was too broken to even check in to a hotel anyway. Could barely get a few words out.

So I ended up here...back where I started.

Pathetic.

When I woke up the next day, it was past noon. I'd slept for a whopping twelve hours straight. My entire body was crushed with defeat. If I weren't desperate to pee and starving because I hadn't eaten anything since early the night before, I would have stayed put. I made my way into the hallway and then the dining room.

Grave's butler emerged. "You're awake." It seemed like a question, but it was worded as a statement and also mixed with a judgmental look.

I was used to this attitude from Hugo, but not Raymond. Raymond and I used to get along, but it looked like those days were long over. "Yes."

"Take a seat. I'll bring you something."

"Peanut butter and jelly is fine."

Raymond looked revolted. "Will children be dining with you today?"

"No—"

"Then don't insult us. You're no longer the woman of the house—and don't you forget it."

"Raymond." Grave's deep voice came from the sitting room. As if he spoke into a microphone, his voice was audible in every corner. "She's trying to inconvenience you as little as possible, and you know that." He emerged at my side, dressed in jeans and a long-sleeved shirt. He must have just come home because he was usually in his sweatpants when he was around the house.

Raymond paused before he swallowed his retort. "My apologies, sir." He headed to the kitchen on the other side of the apartment.

I was in the same clothes I'd worn last night because I didn't even bring a bag in with me. I'd washed my face in the sink and didn't reapply my makeup. Didn't even brush my hair. When I'd left Cauldron, my head was held high, but now, I crashed and burned like a dumpster fire.

Grave studied the side of my face. "Hope you got some sleep."

"I got a lot of sleep." Could sleep some more, actually.

"Some food will make you feel better." He moved to the table and pulled out a chair for me.

I stared at it. "I'm sorry about last night. Hope I didn't ruin your evening."

He walked away.

"Grave?"

He halted and turned back to me, only partially.

"Have you spoken to Cauldron?"

After a long stare, he shook his head.

The disappointment hit me like a punch in the gut. I'd hoped Cauldron had reached out to cope with his own misery. But he'd probably slept like a baby, on a mattress made of my dignity. "So, you and Elise are serious?"

His eyes narrowed in annoyance. "My personal life is none of your business."

"I was just wondering—"

"Then don't wonder." He turned away again. He was kind to me last night, but he seemed to be back to his brooding and standoffish behavior. I never realized how similar Grave and Cauldron were until then.

To my own shame, I kept checking my phone...to see if he'd called.

He didn't.

He didn't even care if I was okay. Didn't care where I'd driven off to. I could be anywhere right now, be in bed with another man, and it made no difference to him. I'd left Grave because I wanted to start my own life, find a nice guy and settle down, and now I didn't want to do that because there was no such thing as a nice guy.

Absolute bullshit.

I gathered what few things I'd brought and entered the parlor, prepared to thank Grave for his hospitality and leave. It was evening, so the windows were lit up with the lights of the city. It got dark so early now that by the time I was ready to leave, it was dark again.

I walked down the hallway to his study and found him behind his desk. He was still dressed in his clothes, like he had plans that evening. I announced my presence by giving a gentle knock on the door.

He didn't look up, like he knew I was there before I even came into view. "Yes?"

I crossed the room and approached the desk. "You're working late." He'd never worked late when I lived with him, unless it was outside the house at a meeting or dinner.

He flashed me a furious look, like he didn't want to be reminded of our time together.

"I wanted to thank you for letting me crash here. I'll be on my way."

"And where will you go?"

"I-I don't know yet." I'd lain in bed all day and done nothing. Didn't look up a single apartment listing. Did nothing except shed a few tears and drown in self-loathing. I should have left Cauldron a long time ago. And I shouldn't have fallen in love with him. So fucking stupid.

Grave studied me across his walnut-colored desk. "Stay."

"It's okay. I don't want to intrude—"

"You can leave when you have a place to stay. I'll help you find an apartment and get you settled."

"You don't have to do that—"

"I don't have to do anything I don't want to do, so that must mean I want to."

I stared at the man behind the desk, feeling like I was meeting him for the first time. He was different than I remembered. "Well...thank you." I got to my feet and left the office, feeling his powerful eyes pierce me in the back like bullets.

4

CAULDRON

Hugo set the tray at the edge of the desk.

My breakfast tray was there, untouched.

He did his best to compose himself and hide his deep offense. "You haven't eaten breakfast in three days, Mr. Beaufort."

My eyes stayed on my computer. "Not hungry."

"Then I'll stop bringing you breakfast until told otherwise."

I ignored him.

He arranged my lunch tray, removing the silver platters that kept my food covered. "Have you spoken to Camille?"

My head turned at the question, stunned that he would step above his station and ask me such a thing.

He immediately cowered at the look on my face. "My apologies."

I turned back to the computer, pissed off that her name had been spoken.

Once he had everything gathered on the tray, he lifted it and prepared to leave. But he lingered, lingered like he was at odds with himself, like he wanted to be stupid and say something he shouldn't. "Mr. Beaufort?"

I was so close to firing his ass.

"I'm sure you know I never cared for Camille."

My eyes were ice-cold.

"But you seemed happy...and now you aren't."

I couldn't believe he had the balls to say that to me.

He turned away when my stare became too much. "Perhaps I spoke out of turn—"

"You did."

He froze at the venom in my voice.

"Mind your business and go fucking clean something."

He remained frozen on the spot, but his hands shook as he held the tray.

"I said, get out."

He turned back to me, looked me in the eye, and dropped the tray on my desk. "I'll just get my things and be on my way."

My eyes snapped wide open.

He dusted off his gloved hands and walked out.

Fuck.

I intercepted him at the front door. His roll-aboard suitcase was behind him, and he had another bag on his arm. He lived here full time, but he didn't have many possessions because I owned all the furniture in his bedroom. "Hugo."

He gave me a cold stare as he stopped in front of me. "Mr. Beaufort, if you could step aside, please."

"I'm sorry I lost my temper—"

"I don't have time for this. I need to go *clean* something."

I'd never been on the receiving end of his sass before, and man, it was venomous. "That was a dick thing to say, and I shouldn't have said it."

Like that wasn't enough, he stared.

"Hugo, you made your point—"

"It's impossible to work for a man and not care about him. If I didn't care about you, I wouldn't want to work for you. This job is intimate, requires me to be involved in nearly every aspect of your life, so you can't expect me not to care about your happiness. And, Mr. Beaufort, you aren't happy."

I gritted my teeth in silence.

"And you owe me an apology."

"I did apologize—"

"You apologized for losing your temper. You didn't apologize for disrespecting me so cruelly."

I dropped my chin slightly, actually ashamed of the way I'd acted. "I'm sorry, Hugo. I was an asshole."

Once he got what he wanted, he straightened and released a breath. "Apology accepted."

"Thank you."

"But I meant what I said before, Mr. Beaufort. You aren't happy. And if you wait too long to do something about it, you might miss your chance to be happy ever again."

5

ELISE

After I dropped the kids off at school, I hit the gym then came home to shower. I tossed my purse on the counter then headed into the kitchen to pull a bag of ingredients out of the freezer to make my recovery protein shake.

My phone lit up with a text. *Sweetheart.*

I dropped everything I was doing the second I saw his name on the screen. Even through text, he maintained his voice, commanding my attention with just a word. *Yes?*

Can I stop by?

The kids were gone, and the nanny was out of the house. *If you don't mind that I'm sweaty. Just got back from the gym.*

You are going to get sweaty anyway.

Only Grave could pull off a line like that. *I'll see you soon.* I finished my shake then drank it as I stood at the kitchen counter.

A couple minutes later, he walked inside without knocking, his sleeves pushed to his elbows, his forearms covered in thick veins that looked like rivers. His jeans were low on his hips, and he took a glance at my white living room and kitchen before his eyes settled on me. He subtly looked me up and down as he drew close, locking his gaze on mine with that manly confidence.

I couldn't believe I got paid to fuck this gorgeous man. Or, I got paid to be fucked by this gorgeous man.

As if he didn't care about the sweaty workout clothes or the fact that my hair was matted and oily, he grabbed my ass and kissed me against the kitchen counter. He squeezed me hard then yanked down my bottoms to spank me on the cheek.

I was lifted onto the counter then he pulled his shirt over his head, revealing a rock-hard chest and abs that I could use as a cutting board. My hands immediately pressed against his warm body as he lifted one leg at a time to slide off my shoes. With my bottoms down to my ankles, he folded me into position, tugging his jeans down so he could shove himself inside me with an aggressive thrust.

Oh fuck. So good.

It was my job to initiate everything, but I never had a chance because he always beat me to the punch.

His arm supported my back, and he brought his face over mine as he fucked me hard on the kitchen counter, drilling me like a sailor home on leave, nailing me like he had never had the privilege of fucking me before.

I moaned and screamed on the counter, on the spot where I made lunch for my kids every day, full of the best dick I'd ever gotten. My hands gripped his ass, and I screamed as loud as I wanted, fucked in a way I'd only dreamed about. "Grave..."

When I came back into the living room after my shower, Grave was on the couch, working on his phone. He was dressed again, the only sign of our rendezvous the slight messiness of his short hair.

"I thought you left."

He pocketed his phone and gave me his full attention. "Not until I take you to lunch."

It was impossible not to smile when he lit up my world like that. I sat on the couch beside him, my arm draped over his stomach and my chin on his shoulder. "That sounds nice."

He looked at the end table beside him where a picture frame sat, my two kids in front of the Christmas tree. "Your kids are cute. Your daughter looks just like you."

"Thank you."

He looked at me again. "They're older than I imagined."

"Like I said, we had them young…"

"Do you have a place in mind?"

"Wouldn't mind some pizza, I guess."

He gave a handsome smirk. "Pizza it is."

It was the first time I'd seen him eat carbs. To be fair, I didn't usually eat them either.

We sat together at the table, sharing a small pizza on the checkerboard tablecloth. Every time someone walked inside, they immediately looked at Grave, especially women. Sometimes the women couldn't stop staring, even though I was clearly with him.

It didn't bother me because I couldn't blame them. "How's Camille doing?"

"Sleeps all day. Doesn't eat."

I took a small bite of my pizza, and I took my time chewing while I processed what he said. "Is she still staying with you?"

"Yes."

"Why?" I already thought it was strange that Grave was the first person she'd run to, but now I found this even stranger.

"Doesn't have anywhere else to go."

"But you're Cauldron's brother. Isn't that weird? Especially since the two of you *just* got on good terms after a decade-long estrangement?"

He took a long time before he answered. "He may not love her, but I know he cares for her. That's reason enough for me to help her. And I also owe her."

"You owe her? Why?"

"Because she saved my life."

"*What?* When was this?"

"Long story. The details don't matter. But if she hadn't stepped up, I'd be dead right now. So if she needs a place to stay until she can get back on her feet, my door is open."

It sounded like Cauldron hadn't been present, so in what scenario would the two of them have been together? I wanted to ask questions, but judging by the way he worded his answers, he wouldn't talk about it. "Do you think they'll get back together?"

"She said she wouldn't take him back."

"Everyone says that."

"Cauldron has done some pretty fucked-up shit, so I think she means it."

"So you think Cauldron will try to get her back?"

He took a long time to reflect on the question. "Unlikely."

"Because he doesn't love her?"

"Because he has no use for her now."

I felt like there was a much bigger story I wasn't privy to. "How long do you think she'll be with you?"

"I don't know." He relaxed in the chair, his arm stretched over the back of the one beside him. "Is this a problem?"

"No. I just... I don't know."

He stared me down from across the table.

"I feel like there's something you aren't telling me..."

Silence. Stone-cold silence.

After I parked the car on the street, I walked to my front door, but I stopped when I spotted the man leaning against the banister at the top of the stairs. A three-piece suit. An arrogant smile.

My first instinct was to walk away and get back into my car, but this was my home, the place where I raised my children, and I would not let some entitled motherfucker chase me off. I marched up to him, knowing exactly where I kept my knife in my purse. "Get the fuck off my property, or I'll slit your throat, asshole."

The smile only widened. "Hard day?"

"It was great until now. Is this how you try to get laid? Desperately stalk women and wait outside their homes?"

That smile disappeared. "This is how I do business. And yes, we have business together."

"You got your money back—"

"But that doesn't break the contract. I signed my name and waited my turn. You. Owe. Me."

I gripped the strap of my purse before I slid my hand down, looking like I was simply changing the grip. "Are you expecting me to unlock the door so you can fuck me on the couch? Then you'll be on your merry way?"

"I mean, I wouldn't say no to that—"

"Get over yourself. This is so fucking desperate, it's sad. There's so many other—"

He rushed me, getting right in my face with a stern look. "Call me desperate again and see what happens."

My hand slid into my purse, and my fingers wrapped around the hilt of the knife. "Go away and don't come back. I have kids—"

"Who aren't home. So we can do this here and now. Unlock your door so we can do business, or we'll do business right here on the street—"

I slammed the knife right into his stomach.

He immediately lost his breath and staggered back. He dropped his chin to look down, to see the pool of red blood that slowly stained his collared shirt, vest, and then his coat. In shock, he looked up at me, his face already white.

"Come here again, and I'll shoot you next time."

———

I put my kids to bed and set the alarm.

I'd stopped using the alarm a long time ago, but now it was back on, somewhat easing my stress. There was a gun in my nightstand. Never thought I might actually have to use it. But I'd made a threat, and if push came to shove, I'd have to keep my word.

My phone lit up on the nightstand. *Get your ass over here.*

On a different night, I'd put on my coat and slip out of the house, but now I wasn't in the mood. I'd gotten some of Kyle's blood on my hand, and I'd had to scrub it with a sponge to get it to come off. *Not tonight.*

I call the shots, sweetheart.

I can't leave my kids tonight. It seemed like Kyle respected boundaries by bombarding me when he knew my kids weren't home, but it still made me uneasy. He didn't seem violent either because he could have attacked me after I'd stabbed him, but he didn't. Nonetheless, I decided to stay put.

Are they unwell?

They're fine. I just need to stay in the house tonight.

Then I'll come to you.

My kids are home.

Didn't stop us last time.

The second he came over, I'd have to tell him what happened, and that was the last thing I wanted. *I'm just not in the mood tonight, okay?*

Now he didn't say anything.

Perhaps it was over.

...

Nope. Not over.

There's something you aren't telling me.

I couldn't resist the jab. *Now you know how that feels...*

What's wrong?

Just had a shitty day. Don't want to waste your time.

Taking care of you is never a waste of time.

Those words cut through all the scars and hit me right in the heart. Men had let me down so many times. It was nice to be surprised for once.

I'll text you when I'm outside.

We went straight to my bedroom, which was on the bottom floor. Christmas was just a week away, and I'd barely found the time to wrap all the gifts for my kids and nanny. I was careful not to spoil my kids throughout the year, choosing not to buy them just anything they wanted, but once Christmas came around, those rules didn't apply.

He stripped down to his boxers, a mountain of a man who made the bed dip once he lay down. He left the sheets at his waist, showing off all his sexy hardness.

I was in a loose t-shirt with my hair in a bun, nothing fancy.

He didn't seem to care that my long, luscious tresses were hidden away in a tight band, that my eyelashes were real instead of thick and fake, that the imperfect complexion of my face was genuine. Whether I looked my best or my worst, it didn't change the way he treated me. It was an interesting phenomenon, considering my ex-husband left me the second I gained some weight—after having his goddamn kids.

Grave cocooned me in his strong arms, the searing heat instantaneous. He brought me against his core and shared the pillow with me. Not a word was said, but his physical presence was more than enough. It chased way all my troubles.

If Kyle were to come back for another round, he'd be dead.

My alarm shattered my sleep.

It was six-thirty, and I had to get the kids ready and drop them off at school.

Grave slept on, not the least bit fazed by my annoying alarm.

I quickly got ready then left the bedroom to pack their lunches. The bedroom door was shut, and my kids would never go in there in the morning, so I wasn't worried about one of them walking in and seeing an enormous man dead asleep.

I dropped them off at school then headed back home.

The house was quiet, and I entered the bedroom to find Grave sitting upright in bed, a mug of hot coffee on the nightstand, and he was reading something on his phone. When he felt me in the room, he put the phone down and looked at me.

"Wasn't sure if you'd still be here."

"Without breakfast first?" he asked, that handsome smile moving on to his lips.

His smile was infectious, and I found myself mirroring it back to him. "How do pancakes and eggs sound?"

"Get to it, sweetheart."

I headed into the kitchen and got to work, and he joined me in his boxers, sitting on a stool at the bar while he continued to write emails and text people. There were days when we didn't talk, and I suspected those were the days he was working, a human mechanic that cut people open for parts to put in other vehicles. Sometimes it was hard to believe when he was so good to me.

I set the plates at the dining table, and we ate together.

With his arms on the table, he scarfed down his food like he was starving. I'd made him three eggs, but that didn't seem like enough to feed a man of his size. His biceps were nearly as big as my head. "Tell me why you were upset."

I'd stopped thinking about it since he'd come over. "Doesn't matter."

He stared at me from across the table, his eyes demanding. "Sweetheart—"

"This is a two-way street. You don't tell me things, so I don't have to tell you things."

He continued his look, thinking seriously about his next move. "My job is to make sure you feel safe. Do you feel safe?"

I couldn't suppress the deep breath that I took. He could interpret situations like a detective.

"You didn't want to leave your kids, but from what I could hear from the bedroom, they were totally fine. So why did you feel like you couldn't leave them?"

I couldn't stand that look. I couldn't stand the way it burned my flesh.

He didn't let up. He didn't blink. He scrutinized my features like a director on a film set. "Has Kyle bothered you?"

Asshole.

"Sweetheart," he pressed. "Why won't you tell me?"

I broke eye contact and looked down at my food.

"Look at me." Now he turned stern, not raising his voice but sounding pissed off.

My eyes immediately flicked back up.

He had me cornered. Nowhere to run. Nowhere to hide. And that angry look told me he'd already figured it out. "What the fuck happened?"

Caught off guard, I was too scared to talk.

"Elise, why the fuck didn't you tell me—"

"Because I don't want anything to happen to you."

That was the wrong thing to say because he looked more pissed off than ever.

"It was my decision. I was the one who walked away from my clients to be with you. This is my problem— not yours."

He clenched his jaw and looked away briefly, like he needed a moment to restrain his rage before he said something stupid. "That's the biggest load of shit I've ever heard. I'm not some pussy-ass bitch you need to cover for. I accepted your proposal, so I'm responsible for your happiness. Now tell me what the fuck that piece of shit did."

I stayed quiet.

"Tell me, or I'll cut straight to the chase and shoot him in the back of the head."

I caved and told him how he'd cornered me at the bar. And how he'd ended up on my doorstep.

Grave looked angry the whole time, his eyes like bullets ready to fire.

"I had a knife in my purse, so I stabbed him. Haven't heard from him since, but I'm sure he survived."

His wall of anger flickered for just a moment. "You stabbed him?"

"Yes."

"Good girl." A subtle look of pride came into his eyes. "I'll take care of it."

"Maybe that was the end of it. You should leave it alone."

"He doesn't harass my woman on her doorstep and get away with it."

"He didn't. I stabbed him."

"Well, it's my turn to have a go." He got to his feet and left his plate on the table. "I'll see you later."

"You're doing this now?" I asked incredulously.

"Yes. Gonna cut through those stitches and stab him again."

6

GRAVE

Kyle had various homes throughout France and Eastern Europe, but it didn't take long for me to figure out which one he occupied. When he was out, I snuck in to his apartment while one of my girls distracted his security team. I made my way into the main sitting room, and one of his servants must have heard the elevator and assumed I was Kyle because he came out to greet me.

Then he turned gray when he realized I wasn't Kyle.

Far from it.

My gun was tucked into the back of my jeans, but I didn't pull it. "Do as I say, and no one gets hurt. You got that?"

After several seconds of trembling, he nodded.

"I'm going to wait for Kyle right here. Warn him—and I'll shoot every one of you."

He gave another nod.

"Take a seat." I nodded to the chair near the piano.

Without question, he did as I asked, sitting by the window, steadily growing paler.

I took a seat on the couch, the chandelier above on a dim glow. The curtains were open, revealing a nice view of the Eiffel Tower. I made myself comfortable and waited, pissed off that he'd stalked Elise to her front door like a fucking psychopath.

Several hours later, the elevator hummed to life.

"It's showtime." I looked at the servant then nodded to the back.

He was quick to hurry off and disappear.

The doors eventually opened, and Kyle stepped out, wearing his signature three-piece suit like he slept in the damn thing. He was typing on his phone as he walked inside, completely oblivious to me on the couch. "Gerard?" He stopped and continued to type, like his message was too important to walk at the same time. "Gerard?" he repeated, as if he was used to being greeted the second he walked in the door. He finally finished whatever the fuck he was doing and looked up. He opened his mouth to call for his butler again, but that was when his eyes shifted to me.

I acknowledged him with a subtle raise of my chin. "Did you need stitches?"

He finally processed the shock. "Gerard, call security!"

"Do you not like it when people show up at your home unannounced?" I asked as I got to my feet. "Because I had the impression you did."

He immediately shifted back. He obviously wasn't armed because he would have drawn it by now. "Gerard!"

"It's just you and me, asshole." I moved around the coffee table.

He moved quicker, trying to maneuver behind furniture to get away from me.

"Now imagine how much scarier this would be if I wanted to hold you down and fuck you in the ass."

He backed up even farther, like I'd make good on that threat. He ran out of room when he reached the hallway. He could keep going, but there was much less space, and it would be dangerous to be the one cornered in that area.

I grabbed him by the front of the shirt and threw him several feet into the air, making him land right on top of his glass coffee table.

It shattered into pieces and cut up his face and hands. He couldn't get up because every time he tried, he was stabbed by shards of glass.

I grabbed him by the front of his jacket and yanked him across the floor, smearing blood along his Persian rug. "Final warning, Kyle." I kicked him until he rolled over onto his back. I planted my boot firmly against his chest and pinned him down. "Bother my woman again, and I'll kill you." I drew my pistol and pointed it an inch from his head before I fired.

His whole body gave a terrified jerk when the bullet pierced the hardwood beside him.

"You understand me?"

His deep breaths filled the silence. He wore a straight face, but it wasn't enough to compensate for the desperate way he needed air because he was scared shitless.

"*Do you understand me—*"

"Yes."

I returned the gun to the back of my jeans and pulled my foot off his chest.

With his eyes focused on the ceiling, he didn't look at me.

I walked into the elevator and stared at him as I waited for the doors to close.

He just lay there.

On the drive home, Cauldron called me.

"What?" I said when I answered.

"What's your problem?"

"Just got my hands dirty."

"Roan?"

"Kyle."

"What did he do now?"

"Fucked with Elise. So I fucked with him. What do you want?"

"Are you home?" There was a bite to his voice, as if at any moment he would explode. "I'm in Paris."

Fuck. "I'm out. Let's meet up somewhere."

"If I drink another scotch, I'll keel over and die. I'll just wait at your place."

I couldn't talk him out of it without raising a huge red flag, so I kept my mouth shut. "I'll be there soon." After I got off the phone, I texted Camille. *Awake?* It was midnight, and she went to bed early, so I figured she'd sleep through the whole thing. She'd probably never know that Cauldron had been there at all.

Cauldron beat me to the house and was in the living room when I walked in.

A glass of water was on the table.

"Well, that's a first." I took the seat across from him.

He cracked a smile, but only barely. "Where'd you put the body?"

"I didn't kill him."

"You didn't?" he asked in mild surprise. "Don't you think that's stupid?"

"Last thing I need is to start a war with the Skull Kings. That would be stupider."

Cauldron had stopped shaving, so his typical shadow was now a full-on beard. His cheeks were hollow too, and his signature summer color had faded to a pale white. It'd only been a week since Camille had shown up on my doorstep, but his haggard appearance suggested it'd been months. "And you really think that's the end of it?"

"I told him this was his final warning. If he does it again, then I'll have to."

"You'd go to war for this woman?"

Without hesitation. "Yes."

"You said it wasn't serious."

"I'm not a fan of an asshole forcing a woman to do something she doesn't want to do."

Cauldron released an abrupt laugh mixed with a scoff. "That's rich."

"I never made Camille do anything she didn't want to do—"

"Like walk out the door?" he asked incredulously. "Live her own life?"

Distance and time had given me perspective, and now I felt shame for what I'd done. "Not the same thing. This asshole wants to treat Elise like a goddamn sex slave. And don't act like you're much better than me. She tried to leave, and you wouldn't let her. So fuck off."

Cauldron's eyes gave a subtle shift, like he'd forgotten about all of that. He reached for the glass and took a drink. "Tastes like piss."

A long stretch of silence ensued.

Since Cauldron hadn't told me he'd dumped Camille, I had to pretend I had no clue. So I couldn't address the elephant in the room, the elephant written all over his empty face. "Is Camille with you?"

"No."

I waited for more, but nothing came.

"If I didn't know any better, I'd say you care about Elise."

"I do care about her."

"How long is this arrangement supposed to last?"

"No expiration date. I'm paying for a service, and I'll get that service until I stop paying."

He took another drink of his water. "I'm jealous, man." He released a light chuckle. "No commitments. No strings attached. No baby talk. Fuck, you're a lucky son of a bitch."

"Am I?"

"No *I love you* bullshit. Just fucking." He kept going as if he hadn't heard me. "She already has kids, so it's not like she needs you for that. No serious conversations. No future. Just living in the moment." It was a drunken rant, his bloodshot eyes dry like he hadn't slept in days. His driver must have dropped him off because he would have crashed into a building if he'd been behind the wheel. "Never thought I'd be jealous of you...but I am."

"Cauldron?"

He'd been looking elsewhere during his ramble, so he turned his focus back to me.

"Something happen with Camille?"

He shook his head then rubbed his palm across the scruff of his face. He released a loud sigh like he was exhausted by the conversation. "We're done."

He was so drunk, I didn't have to pretend to be surprised. "You don't look happy about that."

"I was never happy in the first place. She rushed me into shit I wasn't ready for. Made me a fool for thinking I could ever be more than what I am. Tried to turn me into someone I don't recognize. It was doomed from the beginning, and we're fucking idiots for thinking otherwise." He drank the water again, and when it was empty, he tossed the glass back on the table, where it cracked into a couple pieces.

"What triggered this?" I asked. "Because you did seem happy."

"Now you're hung up on Elise, so I guess Camille's just not that interesting anymore." He sank back into the chair, his skin a little gray, like he was on death's doorstep.

I wondered if I should take him to the hospital for alcohol poisoning. "I don't think that's what happened."

He stared elsewhere, as if he didn't hear what I said. "It was the thrill of revenge. The thrill of getting back at you. That's what made the sex good. Knowing I had her and you wanted her...but that's over now." His body folded with weak posture, looking like an old man who had shriveled into the couch in front of the television. "It's over now..."

I felt no victory, not when he looked half dead as he spoke those insincere words. I'd thought Camille was battered beyond repair, but Cauldron looked far worse than she did. He looked so empty that he could pass away in his sleep just from the sorrow. "Cauldron, it's not too late to make things right. I know you don't want to become the very thing you hate—our father. I know you're scared to change your life. But your life has already changed, and running from it won't fix anything."

Cauldron's eyes were closed.

"Cauldron?"

He was out cold.

7

CAMILLE

Finding an apartment in the city was a lot harder than I thought it'd be. Must be because of the holidays. Christmas was in two days, and not a lot of people were moving at this time. The only things available were apartments to buy, not rent, and they were unaffordable. I scrolled through the options on my laptop when Grave entered the dining room.

Without saying a word, he took a seat and waited for his food to be brought to him. It was lunchtime, so it was usually grilled chicken on a bed of rice with a ton of veggies. Thankfully, I was brought something more appealing, like a soup and salad.

"Any luck?" he asked, his eyes on his food.

"No." I closed the laptop. "Nothing is for rent, only for purchase."

"Why don't you buy something?"

"I have money, but not that much money."

He slid the laptop in front of himself and took a look. "What about this one?"

"It's nice, but I could never afford it."

He ignored what I said and scrolled through all the pictures.

I stared at my food but didn't touch it, having no appetite whatsoever. I'd been here for a little over a week, and I'd already dropped three pounds. "I was wondering if I could talk to Elise about something."

He lifted his head over his food and looked at me. "About what?"

"Work."

He abandoned his meal altogether, and his eyebrows furrowed. "What do you mean, work?"

"I know Elise is top tier, and that's what I want to move into next."

He took another few seconds to process that. "I thought you wanted to start a new life."

"Well...things change."

"What changed?" he asked. "You went through all that to be free, and now you're just going back?"

I shrugged.

"That's not an answer."

"That was a stupid dream. Never going to happen."

"Why not? Camille, you're one of the most desirable women in the world."

I felt like I'd aged twenty years, in body, mind, and soul. "There're no good men out there. I officially give up."

His eyes actually fell.

"I fell in love with someone, and I was just a pawn on his board. Never meant a damn thing to him."

"That's not true—"

"I heard him, Grave."

His eyes widened in surprise.

"I heard something break. So I walked down the hallway and heard his voice." My voice was so steady, like an iron fist, because I truly had nothing left to give. He'd taken everything from me. I was neither sad nor angry. I was nothing at all at this point. "He only wanted me because you did. And now that you have

Elise, I'm worthless. He knew I loved him a long time ago, and he never gave a damn. He never cared how he used me, how he hurt me. And then I forgave him... and he hurt me a million times worse."

"He was drunk, Camille. I don't think he meant any of those things—"

"He sounded perfectly sober to me."

"But you didn't see him—"

"I don't want to talk about this anymore." I cut him off, and it quickly felt like old times, the two of us talking over our meals. "Maybe I can have Elise's number so I can talk to her about getting with her assigner?"

Grave was silent, his teeth clenched like he didn't know what to do.

"Grave?"

"I'll think about it."

If I were going to get back into the business, I wanted to be paid like a queen. I wanted to afford all the nice things I desired. "You know...you were right."

Grave studied me with those brown eyes, unsure of my meaning.

"You said I would regret choosing him over you. And you were right." Couldn't believe I was saying these things, but I was at rock bottom. "We had a nice life. You wanted to marry me and have a family. I didn't love you, but that didn't seem to bother you."

He continued his stare.

"He didn't give a shit about me, but you did. If I could go back in time, I would do things differently."

"You wanted to leave, and I refused to let you go. I kept your mother's necklace as leverage. In Italy, I almost forced myself on you. You're only saying these things because you're depressed, just as Cauldron said those things last night. I know you don't mean them."

"But I do mean them..."

He looked away.

"What if I took Elise's spot?"

He slowly turned back to me, his eyes wide.

"You said it's not serious, so—"

"I know what you're doing, and it's not going to work."

Normally, my body would turn cold at his tone, but now, I didn't feel anything at all.

"I told you there was no going back. You made your bed—now lie in it. Cauldron is my brother again, and I'm not going to risk that relationship just so you can get back at him. I wouldn't drop Elise anyway, especially for you."

His palm didn't strike my face, but it sure felt like it.

"I know Cauldron didn't mean what he said. And I know he'll come to his senses eventually."

I'd cried when I'd heard everything he said, cried like it was the first night all over again. Once my eyes ran dry, I didn't cry again, and I vowed I never would. Cauldron had drained my spirit, had crushed my soul until there was nothing left but tiny pieces. "I'm not waiting around for that. He made his bed—now he can lie in it."

* * *

"Where are you taking me?"

Grave pulled up to the curb and parked the car. "I'll show you."

We left the car and entered one of the buildings. There was an empty post outside, the kind that usually had a for sale sign. He withdrew a set of keys from his pocket and unlocked the blue front door.

"Grave..."

He stepped inside the empty entryway, the hardwood floors shiny after a deep cleaning. There was an open room for a sitting area and a large kitchen on the left. The stairs must lead to bedrooms on the next landing. I recognized the apartment from the pictures listed online.

"Grave."

He raised the keys to eye level before he placed them in my palm.

"You did *not* buy this for me."

He only stared.

"If you wanted me to leave, you could have just asked—"

"After everything my brother and I have put you through, you deserve this. It's a chance for a new life."

The keys were heavy in my hand. I wanted to give them back—but I also didn't want to let them go.

"You can still have all the things you wanted."

"I-I can't accept this."

He looked me dead in the eye. "You saved my life. Now we're even."

"Grave, I did that for Cauldron, not for you."

"Doesn't matter. I'm still here because of your bravery. Money has been paid. Papers have been signed. It's done."

I stared at the keys again, at a loss for words. "Thank you..." My fingers closed around them, and I gave them a squeeze.

"A friend of mine owns an upscale art gallery just a few blocks away. He's agreed to give you a job."

"Uh, I don't know shit about art."

"Doesn't matter. Rich bastards like me walk in and buy expensive shit to put on their walls, and you get a commission for it. Easy money."

It was a great opportunity, but I wasn't interested.

"Do you need help with furniture?"

"No," I said quickly. I had enough money for that. "You've done enough..."

***

We headed back to his apartment, and I started to gather my things.

"Stay until after Christmas. You won't be able to get the heat or electricity on until then anyway."

"Christmas?" I asked, having forgotten the date. There was no Christmas tree in his apartment, and since I spent all my time indoors, I forgot about the holiday season.

"It's Christmas Eve."

"Oh..." I remembered Cauldron and I agreeing to skip gifts, just to enjoy each other for the holidays. I thought we would wake up together and lay in bed for a while. Then have a nice breakfast in front of the Christmas tree with the twinkling lights. The holidays always made me feel alone, but I'd never felt as alone as I did now.

8

ELISE

We made Christmas cookies and watched all our favorite holiday movies before they finally went off to bed. My son didn't believe in Santa anymore, but he pretended otherwise for his sister. I cleaned up the kitchen and the living room before I slipped the presents under the tree.

Like always, my thoughts wandered to Grave. Through text, he told me he took care of Kyle, but he never specified what that meant. When I asked, he ignored me. He seemed busy because he didn't try to see me before the holidays.

I missed him.

As if he heard my thoughts, my phone vibrated with a text from him. *I'm outside.*

The smile lifted the corners of my mouth. He must have sat in his car across the street and waited for the lights to go off upstairs. I let him in through the front door, and silently, we entered my bedroom on the other side of the apartment. Once the bedroom door was shut, he pulled off his jacket and tossed it on the dresser. "Merry Christmas." He looked at me, a shadow along his jawline, his brown eyes dark like the winter night.

"Merry Christmas." My hands slid underneath his long-sleeves shirt and slowly pulled it over his head, kissing him once the material was gone. When our lips touched, it was warm like a fireplace.

His big hands squeezed my ass before he lifted me to his body, bringing my chest next to his. He kissed me like that, our heights equal, his kiss hard like it'd been forever since he'd last had me.

He carried me to the bed and laid me down before he dragged my bottoms off, kneeling at the edge of the bed along the way. Then he pressed his sexy mouth against my aching folds and kissed me so good.

"Oh..." My eyes closed, and I gripped the back of his head as I ground against his mouth, my belly already tight and warm. His tongue was hard against my nub, circling and pressing, pushing me to the edge in record time. It took all my strength to stay quiet, to force my scream into a moan, to keep my lips shut tight.

He was on his feet and lowering his jeans while I lay there, still overcome with how good he'd just made me feel.

His big hands scooped me up and dragged me closer, and a moment later, he thrust into me, his big size immediately sheathed in the cream he'd made me produce. He moved fully inside me, hurting me slightly in the process, but it seemed intentional—like he wanted to claim me as his. Then he fucked me at the edge of the bed, with quick and even strokes, bringing me to another climax just a couple minutes later.

My kids would be up first thing in the morning, but I didn't ask Grave to leave even when it was past midnight. My head lay on his chest, and I snuggled into his side, more comfortable against his hard body than on the softest bed in the world.

"So...what happened with Kyle?"

His body tensed underneath me. "I told you I handled it."

"But what does that mean? He's dead?"

"No. But he got his final warning." Whenever he spoke, I could feel the vibration of his chest, feel the deepness in his voice.

I sat up, propping myself on my elbow so I could see his face. "So you think he won't bother me anymore?"

One arm was propped under his neck as a pillow, and he raised his hand to trace my shoulder with his fingertips. "Not if he wants to keep breathing."

"Good thing the other guys on the list didn't have a problem."

"They all know who I am."

My fingers traced his hard chest, feeling the lines that separated his muscles. "So...do you have plans for Christmas?"

"No."

"Just another day?"

"Just another day."

"What about Camille?"

"What about her?"

"Is she still with you?"

"Yes."

My fingers stopped on his chest, disappointed by that news. "She's been with you for almost two weeks now..."

"She just got an apartment."

"She did?"

"She's moving out after Christmas. Can't get the gas and electricity on over the holiday."

The thought of them spending Christmas together in that beautiful apartment made me feel uneasy. They'd probably share Christmas dinner, have even more alone time together. "Don't you think Cauldron would be upset if he knew how much time you were spending with his ex-girlfriend?"

"I don't spend time with her."

"You live together. How can you not spend time together?"

His eyes narrowed as he looked at me. "What are you implying?"

"I'm not implying anything—"

"We agreed our relationship was monogamous, so what are you worried about?"

When I was the recipient of that steely gaze, it was hard to think. "I can tell there's more to your relationship than meets the eye. It makes me uncomfortable."

He continued his hard stare.

I regretted saying anything.

"Even if that were true, what does it matter?"

My eyes narrowed. "It matters because—"

"It doesn't matter because you and I have agreed that we don't sleep with other people. I don't want her, and I only want you. So can we drop this?"

"I just don't understand why you won't tell me—"

"Because it's none of your business. That's why."

I turned absolutely still, both offended and hurt by his reaction.

He saw the damage he'd caused because he sighed and looked away. "This is a transaction, not a relationship. I'm not obligated to share every detail of my life with you, nor are you required to share anything with me. So let's just drop it, alright?"

"That's all this is to you? A transaction?" The words flew out of my mouth quicker than I could process them in my head.

He turned back to me, his eyebrows furrowed in confusion. "What else would it be? You said yourself that you never wanted anything more. It was one of your rules, and a violation of that rule would result in the immediate termination of this arrangement."

That conversation felt like a million years ago, but it'd only been about eight weeks since we'd met. It felt like this man had been at my side for years. "Yeah...you're right." A moment of clarity rushed back to me. I was a mother to two kids, and until they were out of the house, there could be nothing more for me. This was all I could ever have, a secret lover who fulfilled my fantasies in the dead of night. "I'm sorry."

Absolute silence passed between us. Seconds turned into a minute. A minute turned into several.

"It's late. I should get going."

I bowed my head to his shoulder and pressed a kiss to his warm skin. "Stay." When I lifted my head to look at him again, his intense eyes were on me. "I've become attached to you...come to really care for you. It's made me a little jealous, I guess. I'm sorry I got carried away, so please don't go."

Those deep eyes remained glued to mine, hardly blinking. "I wouldn't slam a guy into a glass table if I didn't care for you too, sweetheart. I wouldn't sneak over in the middle of the night if I didn't desire you more than I've ever desired a woman in my life."

I cupped his hard jaw and kissed him. "I got you a Christmas present." I reached into my nightstand and pulled out a small box.

He examined it for several seconds before he took it, handling it awkwardly as if he'd never received a gift before. He eventually tore through the wrapping and opened the top of the box, revealing a nice watch.

"I noticed you're always wearing a different watch... like you collect them."

He swiped his thumb over the surface of the glass as he examined it. "Good observation." He slipped the watch over his wrist and clasped it into place. "I love it. Thank you." He left the bed and walked to his jacket on the dresser. He pulled out a small black box and brought it to me. "I got you something too."

"Oh...you didn't have to do that." I was so surprised because buying Christmas gifts didn't seem like his thing. I opened the lid and saw the diamond necklace inside. It was simple and subtle, but the same diamonds were flawless in the way they shone. It was probably the nicest piece of jewelry I'd ever own. "Grave..."

"Merry Christmas, sweetheart."

My heart ached as I looked into those eyes, realizing I'd fallen deeper than I ever knew. "Merry Christmas, Grave."

9

CAMILLE

It was Christmas evening. After sleeping all day, I finally showered and got ready. I had nowhere to go and no one to see. Cauldron didn't call or text, not that I expected him to.

I went to Grave's study and found him sitting behind his desk, working like it was a regular day. He was in his sweatpants and a long-sleeved shirt, focused on his laptop just the way Cauldron used to be in his study.

"Want to have dinner together?"

His eyes flicked up like he didn't realize I was there until he heard my voice.

"You know...since it's Christmas." And he had nowhere to go. I had nowhere to go.

All he gave me was a nod.

I returned to the dining room and took a seat even though dinner wasn't ready. I drank my wine as I sat there with my phone beside me, hoping it would ring, but also hoping it wouldn't.

Almost an hour later, Grave joined me. He took the seat beside me, setting his phone on the table like he expected a call. Maybe from Elise.

His staff started to set the table, an enormous feast that was far too much for just two people. I assumed they would be joining us since it was a holiday, and it would be stupid to let all this food go to waste.

When one of the girls came around with the gravy, she bumped into the butler and spilled gravy all over Grave's shirt.

It must have been hot, but he didn't give a shout. He just grabbed the linen napkin and pressed it into his chest, absorbing the warm gravy and the heat.

"Oh my god, I'm so sorry..." She grabbed the linen napkin herself and started to dab at his chest.

"Stop."

She dropped the cloth.

All the staff backed away, utterly horrified.

The butler gave her a nasty look.

Grave got to his feet. "Shit happens." He left the table and disappeared from sight.

Everyone let out a collective breath of relief before they scrambled to finish setting the table.

My eyes went to the phone he'd left behind.

Just sitting there.

Everyone was distracted, so I quickly grabbed it, found Elise's number, and then returned the phone exactly where he'd left it. I finished in the nick of time because Grave rounded the corner in a new shirt and took a seat.

Now, we were alone together, and I tried not to look guilty.

He served food onto his plate like everything was normal.

I got away with it.

We sat in silence together, hardly looking at each other, somewhat friends, somewhat strangers. I was still embarrassed by our previous conversation, when I threw myself out there and not only did he reject me, but he saw my intentions clear as day. "Do you think you'll ask Elise to move in with you?"

He continued to eat as if he didn't hear a word I said.

"It seems like you guys are close."

He lifted his head and looked at me, his dark eyes annoyed. "I already told you my personal life is none of your business."

"I'm asking as a friend."

"A friend?" he asked, his voice slightly incredulous. "We aren't friends."

"We aren't enemies. At least, I thought..."

With his eyes down, he continued to eat, pretending I wasn't there at all.

"Why is it so hard for you to talk about—"

"Because you slept beside me for three years." He raised his chin and looked at me, eyes furious. "Because I asked you to marry me. Because I asked you to be the mother of my children. It's a little fucking weird to talk about my romantic life with you."

"So the relationship is romantic."

His eyes narrowed.

"Your words. Not mine."

He looked down at his food again but didn't touch it.

"You're my only friend in the world, Grave. I guess I just want to hear about your life. I didn't mean to pry. She's very pretty and seems nice. And I can tell she's really into you."

"She's a whore, Camille. She's paid to be really into me."

"I think it's more than that."

He reached for his glass of wine and took a drink.

"Men don't usually keep the same woman for long unless there's more to it."

"She asked me."

"What?"

"She asked me to be her full-time client."

I'd never heard of that before. "Then she really is into you."

"Or she prefers me to the other guys. Can't say I blame her."

"Are you not really into her?"

He looked at me with dead eyes, like this conversation was deeply annoying.

"Based on the way you talk about her, I think you are. So instead of paying her to be your whore, why don't you ask her to move in and make her something more?" He hadn't wasted any time with me. Within a month, I was the woman of his house, and we lived a domestic life as man and woman.

"That's never going to happen."

"Why not?"

"She's got kids."

"So? You said you wanted to have a family."

"I wanted a family with you. Our own kids. Raised from birth. I'm not going to be a stepfather. Fuck that."

"Oh..."

"Are we done with this heart-to-heart now?" he asked in a bored voice. "Because I have shit to do."

"On Christmas?"

"I don't care what day it is."

We went back to eating in silence, our utensils scratching the plate, the darkness outside the windows pressing into the glass. His eyes remained down most of the time, like he was eating alone.

I felt alone. Wasn't sure how I ended up here, sitting across from Grave, in a strange form of friendship.

My phone started to vibrate on the table.

The name popped up on the screen.

The phone slowly turned every time it rang, the vibration making it spin clockwise. It kept turning slowly before it stopped and repeated.

"You going to answer that or what?"

I was in too much shock to do anything but stare. Finally, the vibration stopped. Adrenaline was deep in my body like I was about to run for my life. I'd felt so numb these last few weeks that it was the first time I actually felt alive again.

The screen lit up with a voice mail.

I hadn't expected him to leave me a message.

Grave must have read the screen because he said, "Listen to it."

"I don't know if I can."

"Might be important."

"I doubt it."

He grabbed the phone and played the message on speaker.

There was a long pause because Cauldron's quiet voice interrupted the silence. "Merry Christmas." Silence continued, but based on the slight noise in the background, I knew he was still there. "I'm sorry for everything."

All I had in my apartment was an air mattress and the things I'd taken from Cauldron's. But the heat was on, and so was the electricity. Grave gave me all the info for that job at the gallery, but I never showed up to the interview.

I lay on the mattress and stared at my phone, seeing Elise's name on the screen. I hadn't moved in hours, contemplating the call. After I listened to Cauldron's voice mail, I deleted it because I knew I wouldn't stop listening to it if I didn't.

A text popped up on the screen. Not from Grave. Not from anyone else I knew.

But from him. *Tell me you're alright.*

I'd been gone for over two weeks now. He'd kicked me out without hesitation. Let me walk out of there without saying goodbye. Didn't ask how I was doing when I was at my lowest. The only person who was there for me was his brother...who used to be my greatest enemy.

I didn't answer him.

An hour later, he texted me again. *Please.*

I have an apartment in the city. Got a job. I'm fine.

He didn't say anything for a while. *Good.*

There was so much I wanted to say. That I wasn't fine two weeks ago. That I'd lost several pounds in my depression. That I was worse off than I'd ever been. That I wished I'd stayed with Grave and never met Cauldron. But I didn't. *Don't contact me again.*

His messages stopped.

It hurt that they stopped. It hurt that he listened. He had no idea how much one single text message killed me. All he wanted to do was ease his own conscience, make himself feel better, and he didn't give a damn that he made me feel worse in the process.

I called Elise.

After a couple rings, she answered. "Hello?" The sound of voices was in the background, like her kids were in the room.

"Hey, Elise. It's Camille...Cauldron's girlfriend. I mean...ex-girlfriend."

She took a long pause. "Uh, hi. Why are you calling me?"

"I was kinda wondering if you could get me a job..."

We met up at a café, and she sat across from me in her athleisure like she intended to hit the gym after our conversation. Even without makeup, she could turn heads with that shiny hair and hard body. "I'm just a little confused. You know what I do for a living, right?"

"Yes. But you're top tier. Premium status. I want in."

"Um..." With her hand on her coffee, she tried to think of what to say. "Camille, I know you're going through a hard time, but this isn't the answer."

Guess that meant Grave hadn't told her that we had a lot in common. "I've been in this business for five years. I'm not new to the game. Just getting back to work. But I want to work at a higher level. Grave told me how much he pays you, that you can have a nice apartment in one of the best neighborhoods, that you can afford a nanny and a good car. So I want in."

Elise couldn't hide her look of astonishment. "You—you're a whore."

"Yep."

"So, was Cauldron paying you?"

"No. That was real. Well...it was real for me. Not for him."

She stared at me harder. "I had no idea."

"So, can you help me out? Introduce me to your handler?"

"I mean, you've got the looks for it. These kinds of men don't want a woman who looks like a whore. They want a woman who looks like a supermodel—and you fit the bill. Yes, I can make the introduction. Now that Grave is my full-time client, Jerome could probably use another girl."

"That's great. Thank you so much."

"But...are you sure you and Cauldron are done?"

Just hearing his name pushed me to the edge. "Oh, I'm sure."

Her eyes flicked back and forth between mine.

"He doesn't want me. And even if he did, he's betrayed me too many times. I'm ready to move on with my life."

"Really? Because you look a little dead behind the eyes..."

Yep, I know.

"I just want to make sure this is what you want. Because once you're in...it's hard to get out."

"I know it is," I said. "I need you to do me a favor."

"What is it?"

"Don't mention this to Grave."

"Why?" she asked immediately. "Why wouldn't you want Grave to know?" Her voice changed, a subtle tone of anger in her voice.

"Because he'll tell Cauldron, and I don't need that asshole in my business."

She immediately deflated like a balloon, slowly coming back down. "I can do that."

"Thanks."

She continued to stare at me, searching for something in my face.

I waited for her to speak her mind.

"Can I ask you something?"

"Sure."

"Something personal?"

"Um, I guess. What is it?"

She moved her coffee to the side, like she feared she would knock it onto the floor. "Did something ever happen between you and Grave?"

It was a loaded question, and I was immediately a deer in the headlights. Obviously, she didn't know how I was connected to the two brothers, that I was a prize in a very stupid pissing contest.

Her eyes narrowed the longer I stayed quiet.

Shit.

Grave obviously didn't want her to know. Otherwise, he would have already told her, but he was an idiot for thinking this could stay a secret forever. Grave had just bought me an apartment so I didn't want to throw him under the bus, but I didn't know what else to do.

"I guess that's a yes," she said quietly, her eyes cold.

"It's complicated..."

She looked away, releasing a distinct sigh. "Did anything happen while you stayed with him?"

"What?" I blurted. "No. Not at all."

She turned back to me, her eyes studying my face.

"Grave wouldn't do that. He has his faults, but he's a very loyal man."

"How long were you together?"

I wished this interrogation would end. "Our relationship is long over, so I don't think it really matters—"

"How long were you together?" Her eyes were furious. "You want my help? Then answer me."

My assumption about her was dead-on. She had it bad for Grave. "You're in love with him."

Her eyes were trained on my face like two lasers.

"You don't want to hear this."

"Yes, I do," she snapped. "I asked him about this so many times, and he always deflected. I want to know why he did that."

"Because who wants to talk about their ex?"

"Answer. Me."

Goddammit. "Three years."

Her eyes steadied, and then slowly, the color started to leave her face. "You're the woman he was talking about..."

"I-I don't know."

"He said he was in a long-term relationship with someone...until she left. He offered her marriage and children, but she didn't want it."

There was a lot more to it, but I didn't want to reveal Grave's worst qualities to a woman he obviously cared about. I didn't want to tell her the horrible things he did and risk him losing her.

Defeated, she looked away. "It all makes sense now. You left him because you were in love with his brother...and he was in love with you."

That was as close to the truth as I would let her get.

"And he's still in love with you."

"No, he's not, Elise."

She wouldn't look at me. "I'm a fucking rebound."

"That's not true."

"I've seen the way he looks at you. And why you stayed at his apartment for so long..."

"I had nowhere else to go," I said. "That's all."

"He walked into the bar looking for a whore to make him forget the woman he really wants."

This was going to shit. "Elise, listen to me."

She continued to look out the window.

"Girl, look at me."

She crossed her arms over her chest and finally met my look.

"Cauldron dumped me because I told him I loved him. I went to Grave's apartment because I had nowhere else to go. Depressed, I made a pass at him...just to do something to hurt Cauldron..."

Her eyes remained sharp like daggers.

"And he shot me down. No hesitation. Said I was nothing compared to you."

Her face was hard as stone, her feelings buried deep inside.

"So maybe we had a relationship before, but he's made it clear he's in a relationship with you now. He doesn't want me, Elise. So don't get hung up on the past."

She looked out the window, her arms tight over her chest.

I waited for her to say something, but there was just silence.

I shouldn't have called her.

"You're sure you want to do this?" She slowly turned back to me, her voice delicate like a wilted flower. "Like I said, there's no going back. I canceled my contracts to be with Grave, and I'm still paying for that decision."

I nodded. "I'm absolutely sure."

She searched my gaze for confidence. "You don't want to find someone and settle down?"

I released a pained laugh. "I used to. I thought Cauldron was that someone, but I was wrong. It was a stupid dream. Really stupid..."

10

GRAVE

I didn't see her over the winter holiday. Her kids were home for the week, so I just figured she didn't have time for me. She didn't contact me, so I assumed that was true. But once the kids were back at school, I still didn't get a text from her.

When are you coming over? Her kids had her for a week. Now it was my turn.

That message went unanswered for nearly the entire day, which was unusual.

I felt ghosted.

She finally texted me back. *I can swing by in an hour, but I can't stay long.*

Not a good sign. *Alright.*

An hour later, the elevator doors opened, and she appeared, wearing a heavy coat to fight the cold outside. She took one look at me—and that said it all. She didn't even take off her jacket, like she really intended to wrap up this conversation in five minutes or less. "Did you have a good Christmas?"

I ignored the stupid question. "Get on with it."

Her eyes flinched at my hostility.

"Say what you came to say, Elise."

Her expression remained steady, but her breathing increased slightly. The heavy jacket rose and fell with more prominence. "I'm going back to my old contracts. So...this is over."

"Yeah?"

"Yeah."

"Care to tell me why?"

"I just...think it's for the best."

If I were speaking to a man, I'd scream and throw shit, but that would just make the situation worse. "Can we abandon this shitty act of diplomacy and be real for two seconds? We exchange gifts for Christmas, and now you're here to end things? What the fuck did I do to make you so angry? Be a man and come at me directly."

She looked away.

"Elise."

She wouldn't look at me.

"You think I'm gonna let you walk out of here without telling me what's going on?"

Now she looked at me, her eyes lit up in provocation.

A slight smile moved on to my lips. "There she is."

"I know you're in love with Camille."

The smile dropped off my face instantly.

"I don't want to fuck a man as he thinks about someone else. I don't want to be a rebound."

I held her gaze as I processed what she'd said.

And she studied every subtle expression I made and wrote it down in her mind.

"I'm not in love with Camille."

"Please don't bullshit me. I've noticed something between you since the beginning."

"Where is this coming from?" Last time we were together, we were like gasoline and fire. And now she acted like I'd stabbed her in the back.

"I ran into Camille."

I knew Camille would never volunteer that information, so Elise must have ripped it out of her. "I never told Camille I loved her, so I know that's not what she said to you."

"But it's so obvious."

"You're making assumptions without any context. And even if everything you assume were true, what does it matter? Even if I walked into that bar looking for a woman who would help me forget Camille, how does that change anything? We've had this conversation before, and here we are, having it again. I pay you to fuck me—end of story."

She took a slight step back.

"Elise?"

She wouldn't look at me.

"I'm going to tell you the whole damn story, alright?"

She turned to look at me again, her eyes guarded.

"And then I never want to speak of it again."

Her breathing remained elevated, as if afraid to hear my tale.

"She started off as a whore. But then I paid her to be mine. She moved in with me, became the woman in my life for three years. It wasn't because I loved her, but because I was obsessed with her."

Her eyes averted like a skittish fish in a tank.

"It was about control. It was about status. I decided to marry her and didn't give her a choice in the matter. That was when she decided to leave—and I didn't let her."

She looked at me again, as if she hadn't heard me right.

"*I didn't let her*," I repeated, wanting her to understand the horror. "She tried to escape, and I kept her mother's necklace as leverage. She tried to get it back, and every time she tried, I tried to capture her. So she went to the one place where I couldn't touch her—Cauldron. We weren't on great terms, so he took advantage of her situation to torment me. I knew exactly what he was doing and I tried to warn Camille about it, but she realized I was right in the most brutal way possible. At one point, I stole her back and took her to my residence in Tuscany. Almost did something I'm ashamed of, but her voice of reason stopped me. At the end of all this, Camille fell in love with him and got her heart broken. I warned her that I wouldn't take her back if she chose him—and I'm a man of my word. I won't be second best, especially to him. I walked into that bar, ready to move on. I met you and haven't thought about her since." I paused to watch her reaction, to see if that made her feel better or worse. "Any questions?"

She crossed her arms over her chest. "When did she leave?"

"About six months ago."

"How can you want to marry someone and not love them?"

I gave a sigh. "Maybe I did love her...in my own way. But not in the way where I would ever say it to her."

Her eyes were on the floor now.

"None of this has to do with us, Elise. Why does it bother you?"

Her eyes were still elsewhere.

"Maybe you were a rebound. But you definitely aren't now because I would never choose her over you. You're twice the woman she is."

Her eyes lifted at that.

"Let's move on."

"I-I'm not sure if I can, Grave."

My eyes shifted back and forth between hers. "I don't understand."

"You let her stay here—"

"Would you have preferred me throwing her out on her ass in the middle of winter? I let her stay here for my brother. That's the honest truth."

"You said she saved your life."

"Yes."

"How?"

I released a loud sigh in annoyance. "I can tell you've already made up your mind, so I'm not going to waste any more of my time on this bullshit conversation. Whether I love this woman or I hate her, it should have no bearing on our arrangement. But yet, you constantly let it sabotage it."

"You could have just told me when I first asked—"

"*It's none of your fucking business!*"

She jerked back. This was the first time she'd ever seen me get angry, and she clearly wasn't prepared for it.

"You're a goddamn whore. I pay you to fuck me—and that's it. Period."

Her palm flew through the air and hit me hard in the face. It wasn't as much of a slap as an open-palm punch. "Fuck you, Grave."

11

CAMILLE

I opened the door to Grave on the doorstep. It was raining, so his shoulders were sprinkled with raindrops. His hair was a little damp from his walk from the car to my threshold. His eyes showed his foul mood.

I already knew what this was about. "She wouldn't stop asking me…"

Grave let himself inside without waiting for an invitation.

"I didn't tell her all the other stuff, like Italy and the necklace."

"Doesn't matter because I told her." He looked around for somewhere to sit and realized it was just an air mattress on the floor with rumpled sheets and a plastic armchair beside it. "No furniture yet?"

"They said it'll take a couple weeks."

He took a look around before he faced me again.

"What did she say?"

He gave a subtle shrug. "Nothing, really. But we're done."

"Why?"

"I don't fucking know. She thinks I'm still into you—even though I've told her I'm not. I don't see what goddamn difference it makes anyway. Whether I still want you or not, who the fuck cares?" He walked around the empty living room, looking out the open windows to the rainfall outside.

He had no clue. "Grave?"

He watched the rain fall for a while longer before he looked at me again.

"You really don't see it?"

"See what?" He walked toward me, hands in his pockets.

"The reason she cares so much is...because she's in love with you."

He gave no reaction whatsoever. "You're wrong about that."

"I'm not."

"You're wrong because she made it very clear it's just an arrangement and she doesn't want more. She made a whole fucking speech about it. Until her kids are out of the house, her dating life is on hold, and I respect her for it. So, you're wrong, Camille."

"Well, things change." I'd gone to Cauldron for protection, but I ended up wanting a lot more. "I'm sure she didn't want it to change. It was out of her control. How else can you explain her behavior? She's jealous. She's hurt. Because this relationship means something to her. It's more than a job."

He looked out the window again, as if to dismiss what I said.

"Do you feel the same way?"

He leaned against the wall and looked outside. "I don't want to lose her."

"That didn't answer my question."

"I already told you I'm not looking to be a stepfather. Nothing has changed."

"Again, not answering the question."

When he stayed quiet, I knew he would never answer that question.

"You should talk to her."

He pushed off the window and came back toward me. His eyes locked on to my face before he spoke. "Where did you see her?"

It was hard to lie when that perceptive gaze was directed on me.

"The store."

"What store?"

"The market right on the corner."

"Why would Elise be there when she lives four blocks away?" He knew I was lying, and he was trying to get it out of me.

"She was in her workout clothes, so I guess her gym must be over there." I couldn't believe I lied so effortlessly, but it came pouring out like honey.

His eyes pierced me, seeing the lie but unable to prove it.

"Talk to her, Grave. She may be angry with you, but I know she misses you."

I looked my best before I met Jerome. He must have liked what he saw because he didn't hesitate to take me on as one of his girls. It was a much different setup than what I was used to because I felt like a priceless diamond he needed to guard versus a woman who needed to get to work.

He told me to return the following night for cocktail hour. It sounded like a meet-and-greet, where his clients would have the opportunity to meet all the women in a casual setting before putting their money on the table.

Never heard of anything like it.

I returned the following night in a black cocktail dress. Short, skintight, and with one sleeve across the shoulder, it was one of my favorite dresses. It was simple but elegant, definitely the kind of dress to attract attention.

When I showed up, I realized I wasn't the only one in their favorite black dress. All the other women had the same thought, so it looked like we were all going to the same funeral. They were all young and pretty, size double zero with fillers in their lips. I assumed it would be easy to grab a client, but once I saw the other women, I realized I might be the bottom of the barrel. I was in my midtwenties, but these women looked barely twenty.

We each sat at our own table, and waiters entered to provide drinks and a board of cheeses and finely cured meats. I glanced at the food but didn't eat anything, suddenly nervous for what would come next.

No going back.

The men slowly trickled inside. The first one came, chose the girl he wanted, and then a couple minutes later, the next one came in. It was a slow burn, and by the time the sixth guy came in, the first two had already switched tables.

No one came to my table.

Guess I was too old.

The seventh man emerged, distinctly different from all his predecessors. The others were in suits or sport coats, but this man entered in black military boots, dark jeans, and a long-sleeved black shirt that was pushed to his elbows, revealing forearms covered with protruding veins.

He barely glanced at the other girls as his eyes swept across the room. But they came to an abrupt halt once they found me.

Brown eyes the color of soil after a heavy rain trained on me like the scope of a sniper. His dark hair was styled for a dinner party, a direct contradiction to the rest of his style. Heartbeats passed, and those eyes remained trained on me.

Guess he noticed me the way I noticed him.

He crossed the room, taking his time as he forged a path with those heavy boots. Some of the other girls looked his way, because unlike the other men in the room, this guy was actually handsome. Really handsome.

He finally arrived at the chair across from me and took a seat.

I actually stopped breathing because I was so nervous. I wasn't sure what I felt—attraction or fear.

He didn't seem to feel anything at all. The strained silence seemed to invigorate him rather than cause discomfort. He must have moved his ankle to the opposite knee because his hand gripped something below the table, probably the inside of his knee. He was relaxed but tense at the same time, pulling off both moods simultaneously.

I waited for him to speak first because I honestly had no idea what to say.

He didn't say a damn thing.

I remembered I was the one who was supposed to earn the client, so I blurted out the first thing that came to mind. "I'm Camille."

He wore a look on his face, as if he was saying, *Go on*.

"I've been out of the game for a while..."

"Doing what?"

"A long-term contract." My relationship with Cauldron was so brief, I wasn't sure what to call it. In retrospect, it seemed like a summer fling. Once the cold weather arrived, our heat froze.

He was so still, his chest not even rising with the breaths he took. His body was fully covered by his clothing, but the tightness of his forearms suggested how tight he was everywhere else. His chest filled out his shirt like a concrete wall, and his neck had the same kind of cords as his arms. "Why did that expire?"

"I-I didn't want to marry him." This guy didn't seem interested in long-winded explanations, so I kept it as brief as possible.

He gave no reaction at all.

"What are you looking for, exactly?"

His eyes shifted away as he became lost in thought. His jawline was so sharp, it reminded me of jagged glass. There was a soft shadow along the skin, like shaving that morning wasn't enough to keep the darkness at bay. One second turned into several, and then his eyes shifted back to me. "A woman who can keep up with me."

Honestly, I wasn't sure if I was that woman. His vibe was more mysterious than a black hole. "I don't do beatings or chokings. I don't do chains or whips. So, if that's what you're into, I suggest you go to another table."

"Then what are you into?"

"Me?" I asked in mild surprise. "I don't think it matters what I'm into."

"I don't think you would be in this line of work if you didn't somewhat enjoy it." His eyes were trained on me the entire time, hardly blinking, just laser focused. It reminded me of the way Cauldron used to stare at me. But at least I could read his look. This guy was an utter mystery.

It took a long time for me to find a good answer. "A man who's selfless in bed."

He stared and stared.

I wasn't sure if I should keep talking. "What are you looking for? You're the one who walked through that door."

He broke eye contact again, taking his time to craft his response. "I have a lot of social events on my calendar. As I'm sure you've surmised in this brief interaction, dinner parties and charity events aren't my forte. I want a woman who can deal with all the bullshit so I can focus on what matters."

"So...you don't want me to sleep with you?"

His eyes shifted back to me. After a long stare, he gave a shrug. "That's optional. Not mandatory."

That was the very last thing I expected. "And you want to pay me to do that?"

"I wouldn't want you if you were free."

In disbelief, I stared.

"Unlike these other assholes, I don't have a problem getting laid."

I believed that.

"You want the job or not?"

"Can I know a bit more about you first?"

With a bored look on his face, he said, "What do you want to know?"

"I don't know... What's your line of work?"

He answered the question without hesitation. "Drugs."

He was a drug kingpin. No surprise there. "What kind of drugs?"

"You don't look like a user."

"I'm not," I said quickly. "Just wondering."

"Coke. Meth. Heroin. The whole kitchen sink."

"And...what kinds of dinner parties are these?"

He studied my face for a long time, showing the patience of a monk. "You'll never be in danger, if that's what you're worried about. I just have to rub elbows with men in high places to get my products across borders."

He was probably no more dangerous than Grave or Cauldron.

"Any other questions?"

"You haven't told me your name."

Silence. A very long stretch of it. His eyes were so still, his face so lifeless, it was like he hadn't heard me at all. Then finally, he said a name I'd never heard before. "Bartholomew."

12

ELISE

I couldn't bring myself to contact Jerome.

I didn't want to go back to that.

The first thing he would do would be to call Kyle—and fuck that.

Days passed, and Grave didn't contact me. I was far too proud to contact him and would rather die than make the first move, so I suffered in silence. I suffered the way I suffered when my husband left me for someone else. There were tears in the privacy of my bedroom, tears that I wiped away the second they fell.

How did this happen? How did I get here?

After my kids went to bed, I watched TV in the living room. I was curled up with a blanket, ready to fall asleep on the couch, when my phone vibrated beside me.

I didn't pick it up right away. There was only one person who ever texted me this late.

With my heart in my throat, I looked at the screen.

I'm outside.

I read that message over and over again, even though it was just two simple words.

I know you're awake.

What do you want?

To talk.

We'll wake up the kids.

Then don't yell.

I sat there and thought it through. He wouldn't force his way inside and risk waking the kids upstairs, so I could just ignore him until he went away. But my heart was beating so fast, knowing he was right outside. Six-foot-something hunk with espresso-colored eyes. The only man who ever made me feel weak and made me enjoy it.

I caved and opened the door.

He stood on the threshold in a black bomber jacket, his eyes as intense as I anticipated them to be. He looked at me like he hadn't seen me in years, like I wore a little black dress with no panties underneath instead of the white pajamas covered in little pink hearts. My hair was in a bun, and my makeup was long gone. I looked like shit.

But he didn't seem to care.

I stepped aside to let him in.

He came into the apartment and headed for my bedroom, his massive body oddly quiet. When he was inside, he stripped off his jacket until he was just in his long-sleeved shirt with the fabric pushed to his elbows. He faced me and stared.

My arms crossed over my chest like a draft had come through the window. I stared while I thought about the other times he'd come over, the way he'd fucked me so good in this bed until I saw stars.

He stared like he was giving me the opportunity to speak first.

I was at a loss for words.

"I'm sorry for what I said."

There were a lot of things said that night. I didn't know what he referred to.

"You're more than just my whore, and you know that."

His eyes continued to absorb my every move, my every reaction.

"I could have Camille if I wanted her—but I don't."

"Because you want to preserve your relationship with Cauldron..." My arms tightened over my chest, and I looked away.

"That's what you think?" He spoke quietly, almost a whisper.

My eyes stayed on the dresser.

"I don't want her because of you. I would never betray what we have."

"Out of obligation."

His eyes narrowed in anger, but he managed to keep his voice restrained. "A man's loyalty is only so strong. If Camille was really what I wanted, I would have fucked her and dealt with you later—without remorse. The second I laid eyes on you, I forgot about her. I loved the way you strutted into that room like you owned the place. I loved that fiery mouth and no-nonsense attitude. I loved that you laid down the rules like you were the boss. To see you like this...insecure over a woman who doesn't hold a candle to your flames...is ludicrous. She's a whore, but you're a goddamn queen."

My eyes couldn't stay focused. They shifted back to his face, seeing the sincerity in his eyes.

"Forget about her. I know I have."

I wanted to pull that hard body on top of me and forget these last, lonely days. I'd missed him so much. Stared at my phone and hoped he would call. "I just..." I swallowed, unable to get the words out.

"Sweetheart." His eyes turned warm once he felt my pain.

"You were obsessed with her..."

"And now I'm obsessed with you."

"It's not the same."

"Damn right, it's not the same," he said. "You're far better."

I couldn't believe I was about to say this, not when there was no going back. "I'm not the woman of your house. You haven't told me to marry you. You haven't... taken me to a villa in Tuscany to enjoy me."

His face was devoid of emotion, just reading my expression, reading the anguish.

"You don't feel that way about me..." And that hurt so much. It hurt more than I realized. It hurt a million times more when I actually admitted it to myself.

"Who says I don't?" he whispered.

My eyes locked on his, seeing the first man I'd ever really loved.

"You made your rules very clear, sweetheart. Nothing can happen until your children are grown—and I respect that. So how could I ask you to move in? How could I whisk you away to my other residence so we can drink all day and fuck all night? How could I make you my wife when I have to share you with two other people?"

Reality hit me in the face like a bucket of cold water.

"To be clear, I'm fine with the way things are. We both have lives that require our full focus, so the limited time we have is all we can afford anyway. It's enough for me. You are enough for me."

I didn't realize how much I wanted more until he reminded me that I couldn't have it. It would always be this way, our clandestine meetings in the middle of the night, our dinners planned in advance, my kids never knowing about the man in my life and my man never meeting my kids. It was depressing.

His eyes shifted back and forth between mine. He couldn't hear my thoughts, but he could see the emotions play across my face. "We okay?"

I cleared my throat before I gave a nod. "Yeah..."

"Good. Because I missed you."

Like always, my knees went weak.

He moved into me, one hand sliding into my hair, the other moving underneath my shirt to touch the skin on the small of my back.

"I missed you too..."

His mouth sealed over mine, and he tugged me harder into him, lifting me slightly from the floor so my mouth was easier for him to access. The second we came together, a flush of heat hit me everywhere, my core and my limbs. My hands dove under his shirt and slid up his muscled back, my nails sinking into the skin like anchors from a ship.

He got me undressed as he kissed me, our mouths breaking apart so articles of clothing could disappear. His fingers yanked my hair out of its bun, and the strands came free around my shoulders.

When I pulled his shirt over his head, I felt the satisfied gasp escape my lips. He was so hard. Everywhere. A powerful chest strong like the keep of a castle. A stomach that could break the knuckles of a hard fist. He got me onto the bed, and like a mountain over a valley, he covered me with his darkness.

My ankles hooked together at the top of his ass as he pushed inside me, his big length like a drill to the center of the earth. He invaded me fully, stretching me, hurting me, conquering the land he'd already conquered many times.

God, it felt good.

In near silence, we moved together, my nails clawing into his back as I moaned against his mouth.

His pacing was slow and deep, and he made an extra effort to look at me, to kiss me, to take his time because there was no rush. We had the rest of the night. And the next night. And the rest of our nights.

13

CAULDRON

I drank my scotch at the bar, my eyes glancing at the door every few minutes.

He finally walked in, wearing a black bomber jacket and a tired look. He dropped onto the stool beside me and ordered his drink before he gave me his attention—because booze was more important.

We were the only ones inside, so I knew the stench of jasmine was coming off him. "You smell like a woman."

He grabbed the glass from the bartender and took a drink. "I smell like Elise."

"Midnight romp?"

He didn't answer the question. "You look like shit."

"This is how I always look."

"You didn't look like that a month ago."

Not when Camille was in my life.

"You're running out of time, man."

"Running out of time for what?"

"For you to make things right. Distance makes the heart grow fonder, but absence makes the heart grow stronger."

"What does it matter to you, Grave?" I took another drink.

"Because I want you to be happy, brother."

Brother. He hadn't called me that in a long time. "Her apartment is nice."

He turned to look at me. "Did you stop by to say hello?"

I shook my head. "Not sure how she was able to afford it."

He looked at his glass and took another drink.

"Any theories?"

He stayed silent.

"So, you've seen her."

Grave wouldn't give me anything.

"You didn't have to do that."

After a long silence, he finally addressed the elephant in the room. "She saved my life. It was the least I could do."

A jolt of jealousy exploded inside me, but I kept it concealed within steel walls. "How was she?"

He swirled his glass, making the remaining contents spin in a vortex.

"Grave."

"You want the truth?"

I swallowed.

"Devastated. Utterly devastated."

The self-loathing returned in full force.

"You're devastated too—so you should fix it."

"Nothing's changed, Grave." I wouldn't give up my livelihood for her, and if I didn't do that, she would be tortured and killed just like my mother. I was inca-pable of loving anyone, and that had become even more apparent when she'd told me she loved me so casually, as if it was the easiest thing in the world to say, and I couldn't even stand to hear it.

Grave gave a quiet sigh. "A woman like Camille won't be a single woman for long. She'll replace you. And she'll replace you with a man thrilled to give her everything she wants. Then you won't be able to fix it."

I didn't need a fortune-teller to let me know that would happen. It would hurt, hurt even more than my loneliness hurt me now. When I'd texted her, I'd hoped she would say something harsh, something to make my isolation more bearable, and she did. "Roan is officially in Paris. Now's the time."

Grave tilted his head back and finished off his drink. "Fine. Have it your way."

"He'll be at Heath's party on Saturday."

"And you know this how?"

"Because I know people."

He turned in his chair and regarded me straight on. "What are you suggesting? We have a shootout in someone's house?"

"As far as the world is concerned, you and I are still estranged. Roan won't raise an eyebrow when he sees me there. In fact, he assumes you still think Karl is your enemy right now."

"True."

"So I go and slip something into his drink. He'll die from natural causes four hours later."

"Not a bad idea," I said.

"Untraceable."

"But you can't get caught, Cauldron."

I gave a slight laugh. "This will be a walk in the park, man."

"Don't be arrogant. I won't be there to back you up."

"And I don't need you to back me up."

My brother stared at me with that look of concern I hadn't seen in a decade. "The last thing I want is for you to lose your head because of my bullshit."

"And the last thing I want is for my brother to lose everything because some asshole decided to fuck with him. Don't worry, I can do this."

We stared at each other for a long time.

It's not like I had anything to lose...

Grave continued to study me. "You're sure?"

I nodded. "I don't think Karl is going to be so easy, so save your energy for that..."

14

CAMILLE

The blacked-out SUV pulled up to my house in the fog. It was a cold winter night, the first week of January, a time of darkness after the death of twinkling lights. I got inside, and wordlessly, I was transferred to another part of the city.

I had no idea where I was going.

A couple minutes later, we pulled up to the Louvre. The prism was lit up like a beacon in the darkness. Even the fog couldn't diminish it. Up the steps was a man who stood alone, fused with the darkness as if they were one and the same.

My heart quickened in my chest, not from excitement, but a twinge of fear.

I finally got out, tightened my coat around me, and walked up the steps to join him.

It was a strange meeting place. Not a clandestine get-together between lovers. More like a location for a handoff.

I came closer, recognizing his features once I drew near.

It was freezing out, but all he wore was a long-sleeved shirt with the fabric pushed to his elbows. He was in dark jeans and military boots. He looked exactly the same as the night I'd met him a few days ago.

He admired the Louvre for another moment before he acknowledged me, not with words, but a stare.

"Are we going inside?"

He turned in the direction we were heading, approaching the entrance to the museum. We were on the other side of the prism and pond, and it would have made more sense to be dropped off on the other street.

"When people ask who I am, what do you want me to say?"

"They won't ask."

"What exactly is this? A dinner party?"

"A meeting."

"Like...a business meeting?"

"Everything is a business meeting."

"Well, what do—"

He halted and stared me down directly.

I lost my voice instantly.

"Relax."

Relax? "That's a little hard to do when you're a drug dealer and I'm not sure what I'm about to walk into."

"It doesn't matter what you're walking into because you're with me. You're untouchable. Do you understand?" Those dark eyes burned into mine with the heat of flames. He could burn down this entire city with that look. "Relax."

We crossed through the fog then finally approached the double doors to the Louvre. The lights were on, but no one was around, so it seemed unlikely to be the location of a grand party.

We entered, the lights on as if it was business hours. The walls were covered with ancient and priceless pieces of art, from the Byzantine Empire to the French Revolution. It was all there, preserved in oils and clay.

Bartholomew walked on like he knew exactly where he was going.

I stayed at his side, bundled up in my coat.

After several long hallways echoing with our loud footsteps, we entered a larger room, full of round tables with golden chairs underneath the crystal chandelier. Classical music played lightly over the speakers, but it wasn't loud enough to cover the quiet chatter and clink of wineglasses. There were only fifty people here, more or less.

It was mostly men, the beautiful women only there as signs of stature. The room was warm after the cold outside and the empty hallways, so I let my coat slip from my arms before a waiter appeared to take it away.

Bartholomew turned his piercing gaze on me. "Third table from the left. The man with the moustache."

My eyes followed his directions. "What about him?"

"I need to speak to him privately."

I looked at him again. "And what does that have to do with me?"

A heartbeat passed, and his eyes darkened slightly, as if I should already know. "He's the president of the National Assembly. Despite the second home they just purchased in Positano, she's still unaware of her husband's corrupt ties. You need to distract her for at least ten minutes so I can speak with him."

"Ten minutes is a long time..." I looked at her again, a woman who was at least two decades older than me.

"Since he's a public figure, I have very few opportunities to speak to him without being tracked. I'm paying you a fortune, and I expect a return on that investment."

I started to raise my voice. "You told me you just wanted someone to help you navigate dinner parties—"

"Hence, here we are." He pivoted his body toward me, towering over me in my high heels. A waft of his scent passed over me, and it smelled like a forest in winter. It smelled like snow...even though I had no idea what snow smelled like. "Do this or leave."

I interpreted that to mean I would be fired if I left. "Alright..." I stared at her and tried to think of something to say. My mind remained blank. But I walked over there anyway and hoped that the sense of panic would inspire me.

I reached the seat beside her, and she turned to look at me.

We stared back and forth in silence. My palms grew sweaty. She eventually narrowed her eyes.

I finally took a seat. "I'm so sorry to bother you, but I just completed my education at university, and it's my great ambition to join the National Assembly someday. I know I could speak to your husband about this, but woman to woman, do you have any advice?"

After she processed my words for a few seconds, she smiled. "I would be happy to share my wisdom with the next generation, honey."

Oh, thank god.

She started asking me questions, and I did my best to bullshit my way through it. Out of the corner of my eye, I saw her husband step away. Bartholomew at his side, they left the table and then the room entirely.

It was after midnight when we finally left. The fog was heavier than before. With every breath I took, the air burned my lungs like cigar smoke. We approached the sidewalk, and then the dark SUV emerged out of nowhere, like the driver tracked Bartholomew everywhere he went in anticipation of his needs.

"Did your conversation go well?"

He opened the back door for me. "Yes."

"What did you talk about?" I climbed into the seat.

He shut the door and never answered my question. Then he appeared beside me a moment later and didn't greet the driver or provide directions to the next destination.

"Couldn't you just have one of your men do this? Or any woman, really? It would save you a lot of money."

His knees were wide apart, and his elbow rested on the windowsill. "Free labor is shit labor."

"But there's still got to be someone better suited for this than me."

"Are you saying you don't want the job?" He turned to look at me, his eyes sharp like he wasn't the least bit tired.

"No. I just... I'm not quick on my feet."

"You were quick tonight."

"Doesn't mean that it'll always happen."

He looked out the window again. "Women like you are used to being around men like me. You're used to playing a part. You're used to acting like you enjoy a fat guy's dick up your ass. That means you're perfect for this line of work."

"What did you want him to do for you?"

He looked out the window in silence.

I watched the streets pass and realized we were headed in the opposite direction of my apartment. "Where are we going?"

Silence stretched again, endlessly. Then he spoke. "The night is young."

We pulled up to a nightclub.

Bartholomew got out first then came for me. He cut in front of the line of people waiting outside in the freezing cold and stepped into the cloud of body heat from the patrons crammed inside. The music was loud, the bass made everything throb, and it was so dark you could barely make anything out.

I was too old for this shit.

When the crowd came between us and we started to break apart, Bartholomew grabbed me by the wrist and pulled me to his side. His arm slid around my waist and kept me close as he navigated me to our destination.

We moved behind a couple doors and then went downstairs—into the basement.

The club upstairs was just for show. A business to hide the real business below. I'd seen this sort of thing before.

The one downstairs had loud music too, but it was dialed down much lower. Men in sport coats, suits, and leather jackets were scattered throughout, the cigar smoke a thick cloud everywhere. There was nowhere to escape the fumes. Girls were there too, just in G-strings. They were either serving the men drinks or lap dances or just lounging all over them.

I felt out of place, fully covered in my black dress.

Bartholomew crossed the room toward an area where men had a corner booth. This must be his crew because the second he approached, a couple men got up so the two of us could sit. His authority was silent—but effective.

We took a seat, and his drink was immediately brought to him. She must have assumed I was having what he was having because I got a glass of amber liquid too.

Did I really need to be here?

Even with his men, Bartholomew had little to say. He responded to most of their greetings with simple nods. Then he lounged back and looked bored as he surveyed the room around him.

I wasn't sure why he wanted me there. I'd much rather be in bed right now.

"Are you ready?" He seemed to be addressing me even though his gaze was elsewhere.

To leave? "We just got here."

He turned to look at me then gave a slight nod toward the corner. "I have another assignment for you."

This underground world was not the same thing as talking to an older lady at the Louvre. These men were the real deal, underground criminals that cops were afraid of. I'd frequented events like this with Grave over the years.

"The man in green. Join their table and eavesdrop on their conversation."

I gave him the most incredulous look. "I'm a whore, not a spy."

"A whore is a woman who does whatever her client wants." He turned to look at me, his eyes dead and lifeless. "So you're still in the right line of business."

"I'm not stupid. I know what will happen to me if they figure out what I'm doing."

"You think I'd let anything happen to you?"

"No offense, but I don't know you."

His eyes shifted back and forth between mine. "I swear on my life that I'll protect you. That's all you need to know."

"You should have told me all this up front."

"Would it have changed anything?" he asked, one eyebrow cocked. "You're getting paid a fortune to live an exciting and adventurous life. You get to be one of the boys for once instead of lying on your back."

It was nice that I didn't have to sleep with Bartholomew if I didn't want to. It was an option because he was always game for a good time, but it wasn't an obligation, and that did make him infinitely more attractive. "I want more money."

His eyes narrowed.

"Call it hazard pay."

This guy had no expression other than the one he wore. He never smiled. He never frowned. He was just stoic, always. "How much?"

"Double."

Silence.

I'd probably asked for too much.

He continued to stare. "Deal."

Easiest raise ever.

"Now, work your magic and find out what I need to know."

"What are you looking for?"

His eyes shifted to the men across the room. "There's another dealer in my territory, and I want to know exactly who it is. Based on my intel, a big drop is supposed to happen soon. I suspect this meeting they're having is to discuss conditions, to ensure I don't find out about it."

"Well...don't they recognize you?"

He gave a slight shake of his head. "I only show my face to those who've earned it."

I studied the guys across the room before I looked at him again.

"I'll be here the whole time."

I forced myself to my feet and crossed the room—getting down to business.

By the time we left the club and stepped onto the sidewalk, it was four in the morning.

I was dead tired.

The SUV pulled up and stopped at the curb.

I'd told Bartholomew everything I knew, and he was right. That was exactly what the men were talking about. I'd flirted, acted like I was just there for free drinks, and the guys spilled everything like I wasn't a threat in the least. Naturally, one of the guys tried to take me home, but I pretended to puke in the bathroom.

We got into the back seat and headed for my apartment.

Bartholomew was wide awake, his straight back against the seat, his fingers rubbing against his bottom lip as he thought to himself. Every time lights flashed by outside the window, the brightness reflected in his espresso eyes.

My eyes kept closing, and I would drift off for a second or two. At some point, I slid down into my seat, leaning against the car door with my face to the glass. I fell asleep and was jerked awake when the SUV came to a stop.

Bartholomew took my hand and guided me to the ground so I wouldn't slip in my heels.

I blinked a couple times, my front door slowly coming into view. "I'm exhausted…"

Once I had my balance, Bartholomew released me and walked beside me to the front door. He grabbed my clutch then fished inside until he found the keys. As I leaned against the wall and rubbed the corner of my eye, he got the front door unlocked then waited for me to walk inside.

I made it into my apartment and felt the heat smother me instantly. I turned around to face Bartholomew, to say goodnight, to exchange pleasantries at the end of our…whatever it was.

But he was already gone. The back door shut, and the SUV took off.

15

CAULDRON

I pulled the car over to the curb and killed the engine.

The clock on the dash said 3:38 a.m.

It was dark and cold, with no people and no cars to be seen.

As always, I couldn't sleep, which had become the norm these days. I didn't want to waste hours lying in bed, so I did my workouts in the middle of the night. Once I showered afterward, it helped me get back to sleep.

But not tonight.

Parked across the street, I rolled down my window and looked at the two-story apartment. The windows on either side were pitch black, but her windows still had a glow between the curtains.

She couldn't sleep either.

Or she had somebody over...

But I doubted the lights would be on if that were the case.

If she had someone over...I wasn't sure what I would do.

Not that I had the right to care. Not that I had the right to feel anything but nothing at all.

I'd been in Paris for a few weeks. Cap-Ferrat was abandoned, and now Hugo could do his deep clean of the place. The Christmas tree would be taken down, and so would all the ornaments and lights. I always spent Christmas alone, but this was the first time I actually *felt* alone.

Felt like something was missing.

I rolled down the window and lit up my cigar, the winter cold stinging my eyes the second it hit me. With my elbow propped on the windowsill, I stared at her apartment with no intention of going inside.

I had no intention of doing anything.

Other than sitting there...and staring.

I rested my head against the wheel and imagined a life where I walked through the doors. Just let myself in like I was coming home. She'd be sitting on the couch in her pajamas, reading a book with her hair in a bun, and when she looked up at me, there would be confusion...but then longing. We wouldn't say a word. We would just come together...as if nothing had happened.

I let my mind wander for a bit. Fantasize for a bit. Pretend that cigar was her lips. But then the dream shattered, and I was back in my car, the freezing air hitting me in the face.

Then the lights flicked off. Her apartment went dark.

And that was when I drove home. Alone.

16

CAMILLE

Every couple of days, Bartholomew would text me.

I need you.

He treated me like one of his men. Not one of his women.

After I got over the initial fear, it actually felt nice. I felt like I had more to offer than my naked body. I was intelligent and resourceful. I could make things happen if I put my mind to it. Bartholomew either had faith in me, or he just assumed it was so easy, a monkey could do it.

I need you.

I knew that meant he was right outside. Or his driver was right outside.

I got dressed, even though I didn't know what I was getting dressed for, and got into the blacked-out SUV. The driver took me across town, pulling up to a three-story apartment building that looked unoccupied from the outside.

A man led me into an elevator, and then we stepped out into the parlor.

I knew I'd stepped into some serious shit when I heard Bartholomew's voice.

"My world is built on skulls, and soon, my boot will be resting on yours."

What in the actual fuck?

The man took me by the arm and guided me into the other room.

We rounded the corner into a sitting room, and Bartholomew stood there in his classic dark look with a black leather jacket. His men were spread out across the room, each of them looking unimpressed by the sight they witnessed.

A man was kneeling on the floor, hands zip-tied at his back.

Bartholomew stared him down as he slowly walked over, eyes on his prey.

The man on the floor trembled at his approach.

He stopped, gave a long hard stare, and then slammed his boot into the man's side.

The man toppled over while giving a restrained scream.

Then Bartholomew rested his boot right on top of his head, like a man conquering an unknown land, and pushed down a bit, squeezing the man's head against the floorboards.

Jesus Christ.

"Speak your truth, Bayard." Bartholomew put down more weight, making the man squirm as he tried to relieve the pressure from his military boot. "Choose your words carefully because they'll follow you wherever you end up."

What did that mean?

"It wasn't me," he said in a strained voice. "How many times do I have to tell you, you got the wrong guy?"

Bartholomew went still, staring down at the man with that detached expression. "Got the wrong guy, huh?"

The man's eyes were wide, unsure what he would do next.

I didn't know what he would do next either.

"The. Wrong. Guy." Bartholomew removed his boot then stepped back, arms at his sides, slowly nodding like he was digesting information. "Let's see about that." He turned and landed his gaze on me. It was like a fishhook right in my lip. It snagged me and dragged me forward to his side. "Camille, do you recognize this man from the charity dinner at the palace?"

My eyes stayed on Bartholomew.

His head cocked sideways slightly, his eyes demanding my incrimination.

My testimony would decide this man's fate. I would either be responsible for his life or his death.

He nodded to one of his men.

The guy on the floor was forced upright so his face was on display.

I did recognize him. Instantly. He'd worn a loud purple tie that pained my eyes.

He recognized me too. It was obvious in the way his eyes contracted. Then they pleaded. Pleaded for mercy.

"Camille." Bartholomew demanded my answer.

I didn't know what this guy had done, but I didn't want to be the one to pull the trigger. "I-I'm not sure."

The man closed his eyes in overwhelming gratitude.

The room was already silent, but somehow, that silence deepened. The look on Bartholomew's face was indescribable. He always wore an impassive face, but this was the first break in that habit. He took one step toward me, his heavy boots making a distinct thud. He took another step. Another thud. Then he stopped directly before me, his eyes burning with ferocity. "Fuck with me again and see what happens. This is your only warning." He lowered his voice, speaking so only I could hear the horrifying threat.

Cauldron could be scary at times. So could Grave. But Bartholomew...was different.

Bartholomew stepped away. "Camille." Now he raised his voice, his anger getting to him. "Do you recognize this piece of shit on my floor?"

The man started to shake, knowing his death was sealed.

I had to watch a man burn me with his gaze while another man begged for his life. And this all happened in silence. But I knew Bartholomew was already aware of this man's betrayal, so my lie wouldn't spare him anyway. "Yes...I recognize him."

It all happened so fast.

Bartholomew moved like an animal, jumping on the man on the floor and slamming his boot down into his head. Over and over.

I gave a gasp and ran out of the room, hearing the screams as they followed me.

Thud. Thud. Thud.

Scream. Scream. Scream.

Then the cries abruptly stopped.

But the thuds continued.

I knew that man's skull was stomped into pieces. Blood everywhere. His body lifeless.

I jabbed the button on the elevator and prayed for those doors to open. Gotta get the fuck out of here. Finally, the doors slid open, and I headed for the SUV that was still waiting. I hopped inside, and the driver gave me a peculiar look, like he didn't know what to do.

"Just take me home."

I wasn't the boss, so he made a quick call. He must have gotten Bartholomew's approval because he hung up and took me to my apartment.

A couple hours later, a knock sounded on the door.

It was midnight.

Who the fuck would be on my doorstep at this time of night?

Cauldron was the first person to pop into my head, but I knew that was the wrong answer.

My phone lit up with a text. *We need to talk.*

It was Bartholomew.

Did he come to make good on his threat? *What do you want?*

To talk—like I said.

I didn't know what to do. I was two seconds away from calling Grave.

I would never hurt you.

Not what you said earlier...

I fight men with fists, but I fight women with words. Unless they try to kill me... That's a different story. Now, open the door.

I stayed on the couch.

I'm trying to be a gentleman by not kicking down your door, Camille.

I'd watched him kick a skull in, so I knew that threat wasn't empty. *Coming.* I opened the front door and saw him in his leather jacket. He must have changed because his clothes weren't stained with blood...and other things.

His calm stoicism had returned.

With one hand on the door, I stared at him.

He stared back. "Are you going to invite me inside?"

I stepped aside and gestured for him to enter the apartment. "Are you a vampire?"

"I'm neither dead nor alive, so maybe I am." He stepped into the main sitting room and took a look around, but he didn't issue any compliments.

I followed him, arms across my chest, a little uncomfortable wearing my pajamas around him. "Why are you here?"

He paced the living room for a second, his hand rubbing across his jawline before he met my gaze. "To check in."

"A text would have sufficed."

"But a text can conceal a lie. A look can't." He scanned my face with his intelligent eyes, like his brain was a supercomputer that could pick up every finite detail. "I apologize if my behavior frightened you."

"Frightened me?" I asked incredulously. "You disgusted me. You stomped on some guy's head until there was nothing left. And I'm the one responsible for it."

"He's the one who fucked with me, and he's the only one responsible. All you did was confirm what I already knew. Whether you testified or not, I would have killed them."

"Then why did you make me go through that?"

His eyes steadied before they shifted back and forth between mine. His look was subtle, but not subtle enough to hide the tiny glimmer of remorse. "So my men know that I'm always fair. I always do my research. And I always carry out a sentence that fits the crime. But you're right. I shouldn't have put you through that."

My arms tightened over my chest.

"It won't happen again."

"You won't make me testify?"

"No. But I'll make sure you're out of the building before I act."

I looked away in disappointment. "I feel like one of your men."

"You are one of my men."

"I was okay with it up until now. I'm sentencing people like a judge."

His eyes scanned my face again.

"I don't want to be in that position again. And no, you can't pay me more to change my mind."

He gave a slight nod as he conceded. "I respect your wishes."

"Thank you." I rubbed my arms like I was cold, even though I kept my apartment at a toasty temperature. Without a man to warm my sheets and light my body on fire, the thermostat had to work a little harder.

After he stared at me for a while, he drew close, crossing the distance between us until he was right up against me. It was the closest he'd ever been, just inches away. His scent came into my nose, the smell of fresh snow on the cold ground.

I drew a slow breath, my body ice-cold but on fire at the same time.

He held his stance and stared, looking into my face like he was waiting for a sign.

"Are you going to kiss me?"

He stared for a long time. Let the silence linger like he thrived on tension. He had prominent cheekbones, a naturally stern face, a jawline my fingers ached to stroke, a little bit of stubble down his neck that looked coarse to the touch. "That was your chance to say no." His hand slid into my hair and cupped the back of my neck before he pulled me to him, tilting his head so his lips could land against mine.

My actions were involuntary. My arms moved over his broad shoulders and circled his neck, and I arched my back just as his arm slipped around me to pull me close. His kiss was the perfect reflection of his personality. It was hard, domineering, almost oppressive because he took the lead in every way imaginable. His body had a lock on mine, the kind that didn't have a key.

He was a good kisser.

I liked it.

Didn't want it to end.

But…

It wasn't right.

I had to pry myself away from him and pull back.

He let me go, but the sternness on his face showed his disappointment. The man clearly had never been rejected—ever. He didn't say a word, but his countenance demanded an explanation.

"It's not you…"

He waited for more.

"I recently got out of a relationship, and I guess I'm not ready."

He stared for a solid ten seconds before he spoke. "If you aren't ready, why are you in this line of work?"

"I guess…I thought I could do it."

His eyes glanced at my lips, like the kiss was still on his mind.

"It'd be different if it were just a job. But the fact that you've given me the option…makes a difference."

He still didn't say anything.

And I'd run out of things to say.

"You're in love with this guy." He didn't phrase it as a question, but it came off that way.

"I wish I weren't..."

"Why did it end?"

"He...didn't want to be with me anymore."

He analyzed my face like a shrink on a couch. "Then he doesn't deserve your loyalty. If a woman treated me that way, she would forfeit my fidelity. She would forfeit everything because I don't put up with bullshit —and neither should you. That's my advice."

"You don't seem like a one-woman kind of guy."

After a long stare, he said, "I was once. A long time ago."

"What happened?"

He never answered. "Let me know if you change your mind. I'm always open for business."

I sat in the back seat with Bartholomew beside me. We were in a long line of cars approaching the roundabout in front of a three-story mansion. It was the first time

I'd seen him wear anything nice. It was usually boots and a jacket. But now, he was in a tuxedo, and of course, he looked handsome as hell.

He was typing on his phone, indifferent to the fancy party we were about to attend. It reminded me of Cauldron because work never slept for him either. I wore a dark teal dress with ruffles on one sleeve. Bartholomew didn't buy my wardrobe, so I recycled something from my old life in the South of France. It felt like a betrayal to wear it when I was with another man, but if I didn't wear these things, I might as well give them away.

No way in hell I was doing that.

When we came closer to the drop-off, Bartholomew slid his phone into the inside pocket of his jacket. Nothing had changed since I'd rejected his kiss. He wasn't particularly cold to me, and he didn't seem offended. He had a big ego, but it was also impossible to wound his pride.

I liked that.

The door opened and we stepped out, joining the throng of people making their way inside to the sounds of the orchestra and circulating flutes of champagne. Bartholomew slid his arm around my waist, something he very rarely did. As we made our way inside, he spoke to me. "If anyone asks, you're my personal shopper, and that's how we met."

"Alright. So, who am I spying on this time?"

"You aren't." He handed me a glass of champagne and declined one for himself. "I'm here to meet with someone. Until then, your job is to make this party bearable. Handle all the bullshit small talk. Cover for me if people ask where I've gone."

"Sounds like a walk in the park."

He eyed the people around us with disgust. "For you. I hate this bullshit."

We moved through the party, and Bartholomew spoke with some of the men he knew. He wasn't very good at pretending to belong there. He was stiff and cold, unable to crack a smile to save his life. To keep up appearances, I tried to charm them, taking the attention off Bartholomew and his assholishness.

A very slow hour passed, feeling like an eternity. I enjoyed the champagne until my cheeks turned red, and Bartholomew declined every drink offered to him, probably because it wasn't the harder stuff.

We finally had a minute to ourselves, standing in the rear as the entryway was crowded with dozens of guests in their tuxedos and gowns. Bartholomew stood with one hand in his pocket, surveying the room with that intense stare.

"You see your guy?"

"He's across the room. Trying not to make it obvious."

"Then why didn't you just meet in the middle of nowhere or something?"

"Drug dealers don't meet in private." He turned to look at me, his neck angled down slightly because of our height difference. "They like witnesses. Lots of witnesses."

"So, he's a drug dealer too?"

"Yes." He looked forward again.

My gaze moved across the people, some gathered at the high tables, others crowded in groups. My eyes swept across more faces, stopped, and then doubled back. That dark hair. That shadow on the jaw. Those shoulders.

My heart started to race.

He turned his body slightly, talking to someone with that handsome smile plastered on his face.

Eyes the color of hazelnut. Rich, deep, and bold like freshly brewed coffee. The eyes that still haunted my dreams.

"Shit..."

Bartholomew turned to look at me, eyebrows slightly raised in curiosity.

The adrenaline kicked in, pounding in my ears like a steady drum. All I wanted to do was flee before he saw me.

"What is it?" Bartholomew asked. "You're white as snow."

"Um...I have to go." Before I could move for the door, his steady hand grabbed my wrist.

"You have a job to do."

"Well, plans change." I tried to twist from his grasp, but if I moved any harder, my wrist would break like a thin branch.

He pulled me in closer. "Is there someone here you don't want to see?"

My eyes shifted back and forth between his.

He didn't blink once.

"That guy I told you about...he's here."

His fingers relaxed on my wrist. "Is he with anyone?"

"I-I don't know." The thought didn't even cross my mind, but once it did, I was sick. I wasn't naïve enough to believe he was home alone every night, thinking about me. All those girls on the yacht were now in his bed. Every piece of my spirit had been long replaced by now.

"You want to risk the chance he sees you booking it?" he asked. "Never give anyone the satisfaction of knowing how much they hurt you—especially someone who broke your heart. You stay right here with your head held high. Pretend you don't see him. You're too absorbed in me to give a damn about anyone else in the room."

My eyes were locked on to Bartholomew, but my mind was deep in the crowd, following Cauldron at a safe distance. To be in the same room as him, to lock our gazes, to remember our relationship simultaneously...I craved it. But I also feared it.

"Understand me?"

My eyes focused on the man in front of me once more. I gave a nod. "Yes."

17

CAULDRON

I spotted my target across the room.

Roan wore a tuxedo, but instead of a white shirt underneath, he chose black. A blond woman was on his arm, not a day over twenty. She was either too young to understand the danger she was in, or she cared more about the money, jewelry, and power that came with her position.

The dropper was in my pocket. All I needed to do was walk by and release the contents. There were people everywhere, but everyone seemed to be absorbed in their conversations that I doubted anyone would notice.

I'd slip in and out—and it would never come back to me.

The only thing standing in my way was the throng of people who wanted to talk to me. I even had an interested buyer, but I wasn't in the mood for selling. Once someone asked me about Camille, my mood soured.

If I'd brought someone with me, no one would have asked about Camille, but I didn't want to have a woman on my arm. Didn't want to deal with the bullshit.

I waited for the right moment, juggling conversations while keeping my eyes trained on the prize. Roan leaned in close to his date and said something into her ear before he crossed the crowd and moved toward the other side of the room.

My eyes followed him, but they jumped ahead to see his destination.

A man with dark hair that was combed back. His eyes were focused on Roan like he knew exactly who he was. I recognized his face but couldn't recall how I knew him. My eyes shifted to the woman beside him, a beautiful blonde. My eyes went back to him.

But then my thoughts caught up to me a moment later.

My eyes jerked back.

Blond hair. Green eyes. Beautiful skin that I could still taste.

My heart dropped like a bowling ball into my stomach.

It was like a fucking car wreck. I couldn't look away.

His arm was around her waist, and he turned to her as he brought her close, the two of them exchanging words not meant for anyone else to hear. His eyes locked on her face, staring at her so intensely it was like he possessed the heat of the sun. Their intimacy was loud in their body language, like they'd known each other for a while, like this was one of many nights.

Many, many nights.

He stepped away, pulled his arm from her waist, and then walked off with Roan to another section of the house.

The poison in my pocket was forgotten. The entire reason I was there was forgotten. All I could do was stare at her and watch her sip her flute of champagne. She didn't move into the crowd to make conversation. She stayed rooted to the spot—and waited for him.

Did she know I was there?

Did she know and just didn't care?

I should stay focused on the entire reason I was there, but all I could think about was the woman across the room, the woman who looked anywhere but in my direction—like she knew I was there.

She fucking knew.

Instead of holding my place and biding my time, I made my way over. Had no idea what I would say. Had no idea what purpose it would serve. But I crossed the room, parted the crowd, and walked right up to her.

When I was just feet away, her eyes shifted to me. She was calm a second ago, but now a jolt of alarm spread across her features. She'd known I was there, but she'd assumed I would ignore her the way she ignored me.

Dead wrong about that.

It'd been over a month since I'd last seen her face. I didn't watch her pack her things and leave, so the last time we were eye-to-eye like this was during that god-awful night when I told her we were done. She was thinner now. Her face was leaner. Her shoulders were bony. Her eyes were dry.

Her gaze took in my features with a stony expression, like she felt nothing.

Not a damn thing.

At least a minute passed. Maybe two. The backdrop of music and conversation didn't diminish the intensity we shared. I'd come all the way over here to say something, but now that I had her full attention, my tank was totally empty.

I was furious. Fucking furious. Even more furious because I had no right to be furious. I had no right to feel anything because the reason we were standing there staring at each other like that was me.

When I didn't say anything, she went for it. "What?"

"*What?*" My eyebrows furrowed at her hostility.

"I told you to leave me alone."

"So I can't come over here and say hello?"

"You didn't come over here and say hello. You came over to me and stared." She'd been subdued from across the room, but my presence fired her up like an inferno. "So what do you want? As far as I'm concerned, we have nothing to say to each other, and Bartholomew will be back any minute."

"Who the fuck is Bartholomew?"

She stared me down and refused to answer the question.

That name was familiar. Really familiar. I tried to recall where I'd heard it. The fact that I knew it at all didn't bode well. "Is he...?" I almost couldn't bring myself to say it because it was so horrifying. "Is he a *client*?" Was she fucking this guy for a paycheck?

"It's none of your business what he is."

I couldn't keep my shit together. "It is my fucking business if you're putting yourself at risk."

"Actually, it's not."

"You said you wanted to start a new life—"

"Cauldron." That hot gaze was enough to shut my mouth. "You *dumped* me. You kicked me out of my home. Once Grave focused on Elise instead of me, you lost all interest in me. So if you think you're entitled to any information about my life, you're a goddamn sociopath."

"My decision had nothing to do with Grave and Elise."

"You're so full of shit."

"It didn't." My jaw started to hurt, it was so tight.

Her hand holding the flute of champagne shook, like she was so close to throwing it in my face. "I heard it from your fucking mouth, Cauldron."

My eyes narrowed at the accusation. "What are you talking about?"

"Leave me the fuck alone." She started to turn away.

I grabbed her by the arm and steadied her, and just the simple touch sent chills down my spine. The good kind of chills. The kind that gave me goose bumps all over. The kind that made my slacks suddenly feel snug.

I thought she felt it too because she didn't fight me.

"*Let. Go.*"

I was too absorbed with her to notice Bartholomew's return. I didn't notice the blade either, until it was right up against my throat.

My hand released her arm.

She stepped away, but she gave a small gasp when she saw the knife.

Bartholomew tucked it inside his jacket pocket. "That was your only warning. Use it wisely." Dark eyes locked on my face.

I did the same to him.

He waited for me to blink first or look away.

I did neither.

It was a silent standoff, neither one of us willing to cave first.

"Let's go." She reached for him—not me—and walked away.

His arm slipped around her waist and pulled her close. They moved through the crowd and occupied a different social group, as if our standoff had never happened.

I watched her go, forgetting the reason I'd come in the first place.

"Sir, just give me a moment to notify Mr. Toussaint of your arrival—"

I marched past him and entered the hallway. Grave's study was toward the rear, so I went straight there because it was too early for him to be in bed. He was either working or fucking.

"Mr. Beaufort!"

I stepped into the open door and found my brother behind his desk. Shirtless and in his sweatpants, he looked a bit tired like it'd been a long day.

He looked me over, top to bottom. "You look fancy."

"You know Bartholomew?"

Grave slowly shut his laptop. "I'm guessing things didn't go according to plan..."

"Do you know him?"

"Does he have a last name?"

"He's not the kind of guy who needs one."

"I mean, there's Bartholomew from the Chasseurs. Is that who you are talking about? The guy who runs the Catacombs."

I'd known I knew him from somewhere. "Fuck...he's the drug dealer."

"What happened, Cauldron? Did he get in your way?"

Oh, he got in my way, alright. "Camille was there —*with him.*"

Grave processed what I said before he left his chair and came around the desk. He stopped in front of me, his face contorted as he became lost in thought. "Why was Camille with him?"

"I was hoping you would tell me."

"Why the fuck would I know anything?" he snapped.

"You bought her that apartment. You guys are chummy."

"Chummy?" he asked incredulously.

"I think there's something you aren't telling me, Grave. And you have one fucking chance to confess. *One*." I stared him down, my body loaded with so much adrenaline that I could rip his arm off.

His eyes flicked back and forth between mine.

"Grave."

He dropped his gaze before he spoke. "She came straight here. Needed a place to stay."

All the air left my lungs.

"She stayed for two weeks."

"You were shacked up with my girl for two weeks?" Maybe I really would rip his arm off.

"*Your* girl?" An eyebrow cocked up his face. "If she were your girl, she wouldn't have needed to come to me in the first place. She drove straight here because she was so depressed, she didn't even know how to take care of herself. Didn't know how to check in to a hotel. So, yes, I let her stay here. And the only thing I should be hearing from you is thank you."

"How long did she stay?"

"Two weeks. I just told you that."

"So she was here for Christmas?"

"Yes."

I wasn't sure what made me more jealous. Grave or Bartholomew. "Did you fuck her?"

Grave withdrew slightly, his eyes narrowed in deep offense. "Elise is my woman, and I've always been a one-woman kind of guy."

"You didn't answer my question—"

"Fuck you, Cauldron. Of course I didn't sleep with her. She made her bed—now she can lie in it. You think I desire her whatsoever after she made her decision? No, asshole. I'm better than that. I deserve better than that. Elise is all over me every chance she gets. That woman makes me feel like more of a man than Camille ever did."

I looked away, my rage still pent-up with no avenue for release. "Why didn't you tell me?"

"Because she asked me not to."

"Why wouldn't she want me to know?"

"Maybe because she has some pride?" he suggested. "Didn't want you to know just how badly you hurt her. Can't say I blame her. She's always been proud."

"She said I didn't want her anymore because you moved on—and she heard it straight from my mouth. What's she talking about?"

"Remember that night you stopped by?" he said. "You woke up on my couch?"

"I remember waking up..."

"You went on a long rant about her, and that's what you said."

I had no recollection of it. "And she heard every word?"

"Yes."

"A little heads-up would have been nice."

"You were so drunk, you probably wouldn't have understood a word I said."

"I don't remember saying that, and if I did say it, I didn't mean it."

"I told her you were drunk, but she didn't believe me. Said you sounded sober, but she couldn't see you."

Fuck, this was a nightmare.

"But in the end, what does it really matter?" he asked. "You're done."

If we were done, why did it hurt so much? "Is Camille working as a whore again?"

"I have no idea, Cauldron. I got her a job at an art gallery, but I guess she didn't take it."

I needed to know. Was this guy a client—or someone she actually cared for?

"Why didn't you ask her?"

"Because she hates me," I said. "And Bartholomew put a knife to my throat."

"Then I guess that means you didn't deal with Roan."

"No."

He didn't seem angry about it.

"He and Bartholomew know each other."

"That makes sense since Bartholomew is the biggest dealer in France."

I stepped away, sheer pain consuming my body. "I can't believe she's fucking a drug lord."

"I sell organs on the black market, so it's not much of a stretch." Grave took a seat on the couch and uncorked the decanter before he poured himself a glass.

I dropped into the armchair and yanked my tie until it came free.

He poured me a glass and slid it across the table toward me.

I was too depressed to drink—a new low for me. "I need to know if she's working again."

"What does it matter, Cauldron?" He took a drink then leaned back into the couch.

"All she wanted was to start over, find a nice guy, settle down. She had it... But then she went back...because of me." I knew it was because of me. She'd forfeited her chance at happiness because she didn't believe in happiness anymore.

"You don't know that. Maybe she bumped into Bartholomew and they hit it off."

He was tall and handsome. Had features as sharp as glass. Had as much money as I did. The ultimate competition. "I need to know."

"Again, what does it matter?"

"It matters because..." I looked at the floor, unable to get the words out because I wasn't sure what those words were. "I fucked up. I fucked up, and I have to make it right."

The look he gave me was one of pure loathing. "Please tell me you aren't serious."

I held that stare as long as I could before I looked away.

"I warned you. I fucking warned you. Now it's too late."

I closed my eyes, not wanting to hear it.

"If Bartholomew is a client, she's stuck. So it's not like she can get out of it at this point, even if she wanted to. And if they're in a real relationship, she's also stuck, because I doubt Bartholomew would let her walk away without a fight."

Fuck, man. "He seemed to know exactly who I was..."

"That means she told him you broke her heart. That means pillow talk. And that means what they have is real. I'm sorry, Cauldron. Looks like you're too late."

I bowed my head, my fingers pushing up the side of my face as I gave a heavy sigh.

"Elise and I had our problems. She walked out on me."

My eyes stayed on the floor as I listened.

"It only took me a couple days to get off my ass and get her back."

I raised my head fully and looked at him.

"I told you not to wait too long."

I was outside her apartment again, but this time, I didn't intend to stay in the car. As far as I could tell, she was alone. The lights were on throughout the house, and I occasionally saw a single silhouette pass across the curtains.

I made my move and headed to her front door. I grabbed the handle and intended to walk inside like I owned the place, but I steadied myself when reality kicked in. My fist moved to the door instead, and I knocked.

I heard her footsteps. Noticed the shadow behind the peephole. Knew she stared right at my face with annoyance in her heart. Ignoring me wasn't an option because I knew she was home.

The lock finally turned, and the door swung in.

Those green eyes used to light up a goddamn room when they looked at me. Her smile used to be subtle but carried so much affection. But now, she looked like a stone statue, gray and lifeless, irritated by my presence.

It was a kick to the nuts every time.

"What part of leave me the fuck alone don't you understand?" She didn't raise her voice, but her anger was so loud, it split my eardrums. "What do you want, Cauldron?"

"I just want to talk—"

"About?" She kept one hand on the door, prepared to slam it in my face. "I have nothing to say to you."

"Let's talk inside, Camille."

"Fuck off, Cauldron." She yanked the door shut.

I slipped my shoe inside and jammed the door.

She looked like she wanted to kill me. She actually shoved me in the chest.

I hardly moved.

"So this is how it is?" She raised her voice, indifferent to the people who passed on the street. "We talk when *you* want to talk? I move out when *you* don't want me there? Everything is based on your bullshit?"

This was hate. Straight-up hate. Made me feel like shit.

She shoved the door as hard as she could so it flung outward and slammed into the side of the house. "Fine. Oh, won't you please come in?" She gave a dramatic bow then stormed into the house, past the staircase to a sitting room in the rear.

I lingered on the threshold, unsure if there was any point to this conversation when she was so livid. I finally shut the door behind me and joined her in the sitting room.

With her arms crossed over her chest, she stood near one of the windows. Her apartment was sparse, just a couple couches with a TV propped up on a coffee table. There was no rug or wall décor. She was in a long-sleeved shirt and jeans, her feet bare on the hardwood. "The sooner you talk, the sooner you leave. So, say what you want to say."

I wasn't even entirely sure why I'd come all the way here. Wasn't sure what I hoped to achieve when I could see how much she hated me. What we had together was long gone—because I burned it to the ground. "Are you back to your old profession?"

She stilled at the question, as if she expected me to say something else. "What?"

"Are you fucking men for money?" I could barely bring myself to say it.

Her eyes slowly narrowed. "What business is it of yours?"

"It's my business because you wanted to be free. You wanted to start over. Meet a nice guy. Settle down and have some kids. But if you're back at ground zero, then why the fuck did you leave me in the first place? Why did you demand more of me when you would have settled for less?"

She was absolutely still, almost as if she didn't hear what I'd just said. "So that's what you came all the way down here to say? That you wish I were still your *whore*?"

That came out harsher than I'd meant. "Are you back in the game or not?"

"Why do you think I'm obligated to cooperate with this interrogation? We haven't spoken in a month, we're strangers now, and yet, you think you're entitled to my privacy. What the fuck is wrong with you?"

"Just answer the goddamn question—"

"Yes." She threw her arms up. "I'm back in the game. Bartholomew is my first client. Happy?"

It was like a blade sliced across my throat. I could feel the blood drip down and soak into my shirt. "Do you have any idea who he is—"

"Dangerous drug lord. Yes, I know exactly who he is."

"What happened, Camille?" I asked in desperation. "You said you wanted a family. You said you wanted more out of life." If she could accept this superficial lifestyle, why couldn't she accept it with me?

"What happened?" she asked as she raised her voice. "Reality check. That's what happened. There's no such thing as a good guy. Men are all dogs. Some are just better at hiding it than others. I was never going to find a husband. I was never going to find a man who would treat me right, especially after knowing about my past. It was a stupid dream. And kids? Why would I want to bring kids into this fucked-up world? Why would they want a mother who used to be a whore for a living?"

I knew I was responsible for all of this. I didn't just break her heart. I shattered her spirit.

She stared at me as she waited for me to respond to her heartbreaking words.

"I'm sorry."

"Sorry for what?"

"Everything."

She looked away, brushing off my sincerity like it meant nothing to her.

"I've been miserable since the moment you left."

She gave no reaction. It was as if she didn't hear me.

"Thought about you every moment we've been apart."

She gave an audible sigh. "And yet, the only reason you show your face is when I'm with someone else."

"It didn't feel good... I'll admit that." It still hurt. Images of them together popped into my head against my will and made me sick. Just the thought of him touching her...corroded my heart.

She continued to look out the window, the corners of the glass gray with fog.

I came close, crossing the distance between us until we were just feet apart.

She turned to look at me.

"Come home." The words came out on their own. I didn't think. Just acted. Rode with my emotions. "Leave him. Sell the apartment. And come home."

She gave no reaction whatsoever. "No."

The air left my lungs like she'd squeezed them both in her iron grasp. "Baby—"

"I'm not your baby." She spoke without emotion. Her voice was monotone, like she'd never feel anything again. "Not anymore. I'm never coming back, so don't ask me again."

"Camille—"

"You only want me because you can't have me."

"That's not true—"

"It is true," she said coldly. "You wanted me because Grave wanted me, then dumped me when he found Elise. Now I'm with Bartholomew, and your entitled ego can't stand the fact that someone else wants me."

"Camille, that's not what happened—"

"I heard you, asshole."

"I was drunk off my ass and so depressed I almost drove my car into a building. Don't take those words at face value."

"Even if I believed you, I'm done giving you chances. You've stabbed me in the back way too many times. Fool me once, shame on you. Fool me twice, shame on me. In our case, it would be *three* times. Love made me blind, but not anymore."

"It'll be different this time—"

"No, it won't," she said with a laugh. "You've had a full month to come get me, and you never did. And you *never* would have come if you didn't see me with someone else. The fact that Bartholomew is one fine piece of man just pissed you off even more. You know what? I'm glad you saw us together. Maybe now you understand that just because I'm worthless to you doesn't mean I'm worthless to other people."

Her words were a punch that broke my nose. "I don't think you're worthless. But I've come to realize how worthless I am without you."

Her eyes didn't soften. She didn't melt. Nothing.

My words literally had no effect.

"You must know that I stayed with Grave over the holidays."

The thought of them alone together for weeks made me insane, even when I had no right to be.

"I went straight to him because I didn't know what else to do. I was so broken that all rational thought left my body. He let me stay in a guest room, and I spent those two weeks sleeping and crying...then sleeping and crying some more." With her arms crossed over her chest, she cocked her head slightly. "Even made a pass at him, just to hurt you."

I did my best to keep a straight face, but I knew my eyes betrayed me.

"He turned me down."

Grave had failed to mention all of that.

"You've hurt me more than anyone else I've ever met. The fact that you're here is such a slap in the face. To come here and try to fuck with me *again*..."

"I'm not fucking with you—"

"Go home, Cauldron. Go back to your girls on your yacht. I don't want to see your face ever again."

"I haven't been with anyone else."

Her look was so subtle that I could have missed it if I had blinked. It was a slight shift in her eyes, a softness that faded the tension set in her face. It was a tiny glimmer of hope, but hope, nonetheless.

I still had a chance.

"Get out of my apartment," she said. "And don't come back."

18

ELISE

The restaurant was quiet. Couples talking among themselves. Cutlery lightly tapping against the dishes. Candlelight casting small shadows across the room. Grave reached for his wineglass and took a drink.

Every movement he made was sexy, from the delicate way he handled the glass in his hand to the way he rubbed his callused fingers over his three-day shadow. He was in an olive-green long-sleeved shirt, my favorite color on him. It complemented his dark features, his tanned skin and espresso-colored eyes. He seemed to notice the intensity of my stare because he met my gaze and didn't look away.

God, this man was fiiiine.

"What are you thinking about?" he asked.

I was too embarrassed to say it, so I grabbed my glass and looked at the contents. "That you're a hunk." I took a drink and kept my gaze averted, but I felt his hot stare on my face. All I ever did was compliment this man. I should be smart and keep my cards close to my chest, but all my feelings spilled out every time I was with him. When I finally had the courage to look at him again, he wore a slight smile.

Silence passed between us for a while. The waiter brought our meal, and of course, Grave had ordered the biggest steak on the menu. We dined in silence, the two of us at a place in our relationship where a conversation wasn't necessary.

After a while, he spoke. "Cauldron suspects Camille has returned to her former line of work. I got her a cushy job as a sales associate at an art gallery, but when I called down there, they said she never showed up."

He didn't ask me a question, but he was definitely interrogating me. He had that way about him, to say one thing but imply something else.

That thunderous gaze settled on me, piercing through flesh and bone to the soul underneath.

I stayed quiet.

"Elise."

"Yes?"

His eyes narrowed farther. "I know you didn't run into her at the market."

I told her I'd keep her secret safe, but it seemed like the brothers had figured it out.

"You introduced her to Jerome, didn't you?"

I gave a loud sigh, and that was my confession of guilt. "The woman can do whatever she wants. She doesn't owe Cauldron a damn thing."

"I never said she did."

"It's none of your business. It's none of Cauldron's business either."

"He ran into her at a party. Saw her new client. Bartholomew. You know who that is?"

I grabbed my wineglass and took a drink. "Just because I'm a whore doesn't mean I know all the players in town."

"Elise."

"No, I don't know him."

"Then consider yourself lucky because the asshole is dangerous."

"Camille knew what she was getting herself into."

"Or she was just too depressed to understand what she was getting herself into."

Camille was a nice girl and I felt no ill will toward her, but whenever I listened to Grave talk about her, an ugly monster reared up from inside my chest. I got jealous every single time, knowing how much she had meant to him. "I don't think Cauldron has the right to care, not after what he did."

Grave turned silent, cutting into his meat and slowly eating it, piece by piece. "I agree. But I still feel bad for him. I know he cares for her, and despite the way she acts, I know she cares for him. If Cauldron just got his shit together, his life wouldn't be so fucked up. The guy has issues. Serious issues."

"Like what?"

He gave me a long stare.

"Sorry. Didn't mean to pry."

"It's not my story to tell."

"So...you aren't mad at me because I introduced her to Jerome?"

After he chewed his bite, he shook his head. "No. She was going to do it whether you helped her or not. I just wish her response to heartache wasn't self-destruction."

"Being a whore isn't self-destructive. It provides wealth that I wouldn't be able to attain otherwise. She told me that's what drew her to the job in the first place. She knows I have a beautiful apartment, a Range Rover, and a nanny. Instead of giving her goods away for free to a man who cut her down, she wants some serious money. Can't say I blame her."

He continued to eat, remaining silent for the rest of the meal. When the bill came, he paid it, and then we drove to his apartment a few blocks away. The second we walked inside, I was surrounded by his presence, the place that had become a second home to me. Decorated in masculine elegance, it reflected his spirit perfectly.

He took my jacket off my shoulders before he headed to his bedroom. The fire was already burning in the fireplace, the fog pressed up against the windows with the curtains drawn.

On the bed was a sexy ensemble, crotchless bottoms and a lacy bra that would barely cover my breasts.

Wordlessly, he undressed then lay on top of the bed, muscular and naked, his semi-hard dick lying against his stomach. His fingers locked together behind his head, and he stared at me, silently asking me to try on the piece waiting for me.

This was the first time he'd done something like that. It was usually straight down to business, regardless of what I wore, even my white pajamas with the little pink hearts. I took it into the bathroom and changed, donning the two pieces as well as the black stockings.

When I came back into the room, he was already hard, like he was imagining how I'd look in the lingerie and how he'd fuck me as I wore it. He sat there and looked me up and down, wearing a hard gaze that could cut through steel.

His stare was hotter than the sun.

He abruptly left the bed then came toward me, a mountain to my valley, and then came behind me, his hands grabbing on to my hips as he dipped his lips to my shoulder. He pressed a kiss to my skin. Then another. He moved to my collarbone before caressing my neck with kisses, before inhaling my scent with a masculine groan of approval. His big hands started to grip me, holding on to my hips before squeezing my tits in the delicate fabric.

I pressed up against him and breathed, letting him devour me as I stood there, his dick as hard as a rod against my back. I was the one who was supposed to strip and give him a lap dance before I sucked his big dick and acted like it was the most fun I'd ever had. But he was the one pleasing me, making me short of breath, making me feel like I'd never really been touched by a man.

He lifted my knees onto the bed, my ass in the air at the edge.

Then I heard him lower himself to his knees, his face right in my pussy. His breaths fell across my skin before I felt that powerful tongue swipe my most sensitive place. His nose slid in, breathing in my scent before he kissed me, kissed my pussy like she would kiss him back.

I could see my reflection in the glass of his windows, his broad shoulders sticking out from either side of my hips. I could see the redness of my face, see the way I enjoyed what that powerful mouth was doing to me.

Then he moved farther up—and kissed me there.

There.

I gave a quiet gasp when I felt his tongue swipe over me. Then his tongue burrowed inside me, forcing me open so I could receive his wet kiss. That was when I started to grip the comforter and quiver, aroused but also nervous. He'd never kissed me there before. Never plunged his tongue inside me.

I knew what would come next.

A finger. Then two.

And then...

He'd fuck me in the ass.

Just as I predicted, that happened. Except I got three fingers instead of two. I breathed hard as he opened me up wider, keeping me wet and relaxed as he rubbed my clit with his other hand.

This wasn't my first time. But this man had one hell of a dick.

He got to his feet, and then I heard his nightstand open and close. When he came back, he stayed on his feet, and then a splash of lube squirted onto my ass. He rubbed it across both cheeks before his fingers slipped back inside and spread it where my body needed it most.

Then I heard him squirt himself.

Oh fuck, this was going to hurt.

He grabbed one of my hips with his slippery hand then pointed his head inside my entrance. It was like squeezing a sponge into a garden hose. No amount of pressure would make it fit.

"Come on, sweetheart..." His fingers rubbed my clit harder as he kept his dick right at my entrance.

I slowly opened and allowed a little more inside.

"Attagirl."

"I-I wasn't expecting this."

He slid it a little farther inside, and that was when it really started to hurt.

"With an ass like this?" He pushed a little farther inside. "Don't be naïve." Farther and farther he inched until he was completely inside me.

I breathed through the pain, feeling like there was a flashlight up my ass. "God..."

He started to thrust, fucking me in the ass without mercy.

"Grave, slow down."

It took him a second to obey, like he enjoyed it too much to stop. "I thought you'd be a pro at this."

"Well, you've got a big dick."

His grin was audible through his words. "You got me there, sweetheart."

"I-I didn't think you'd want to do something like this."

He held on to both of my hips and thrust into me slowly, keeping it as gentle as possible. "I may like you, Elise. But I'm still a paying customer and you're a whore, so you bet your ass I'm going to fuck you like one."

It was my favorite way to wake up. Cocooned in the arms of this man. I was warm and safe, and the winter sun came through the open curtains and gently aroused me with its kiss. My eyes slowly opened, seeing the top of his chest right up against my nose.

I wished I could do this every day.

He seemed to be waiting for me to wake up because he pressed a kiss to my forehead. "Morning, sweetheart."

"Morning..."

He always waited for me to wake up before he got out of bed and started his day. He threw on gym shorts and a t-shirt before he slipped on his running shoes. He was going to hit the gym like he did every morning, just an hour later than usual.

I forced myself out of bed and put my clothes back on. I always performed the walk of shame when I left his house, but my kids were at school so they never saw me. In my black dress and heels, it was obvious I'd slept in someone else's bed.

"You're welcome to leave a couple things here—if you want."

"I am?"

He walked over to his dresser and pulled open the third drawer. It was empty, like he'd moved stuff around to create space.

I smiled. "Thanks. I'll consider it."

"You want some breakfast before you go?" he asked as he guided me into the hallway and back to the main room.

"No. I've got too much to do today."

He gave me a kiss by the elevator then said goodbye.

After I left, I headed to the bar to grab my money from Jerome. It was before seven, so the place was still open. When I walked inside, hardly anyone was there, including Kyle, and I headed to the office in the back to collect my money for the work I would gladly do for free.

Camille was already there. Jerome handed her a wad of cash that stressed the corners of the white envelope. It must be her first payment because she tested the weight of the money and examined it like she'd never seen so much cash before.

"Your first payday, huh?" I walked over, hoping my large jacket would hide the wrinkles in my dress.

Camille looked at me before she held up the money. "Yep. Should have brought a bigger purse..."

I entered the office and grabbed my cash before I walked out with Camille. "So, how are things going with Bartholomew?"

She stilled at the sound of his name, her eyes narrowed in confusion.

"Grave told me," I explained. "He also said the guy is dangerous."

"He definitely is—but not to me."

We made it outside, the cold winter air surrounding us and making our breath escape as fog. "I guess that mean things are going well?"

"I'd say so," she said. "I like him."

We stood together at the curb, our cars parked at the sidewalk. "That's good. I know getting into this line of work can be a hard adjustment, but it seems like you're adapting well."

She gave a shrug.

I assumed she was still in love with Cauldron, even if she didn't say it out loud, so it must be hard to have a new client, a man you didn't even know.

"Cauldron saw us together at a party. Now he won't leave me alone."

"What does he want?"

"I'm not entirely sure," she said. "He says he wants me back, but I don't think he even knows what he wants."

I saw the sadness in her eyes—and the rage.

"He doesn't want me, but he doesn't want anyone else to want me either."

"Maybe seeing you with someone else is a wake-up call for him."

"No," she said. "It's just a reminder that he only wants what he can't have..."

19

GRAVE

"Mr. Toussaint, your brother is here to see you."

I looked up from my desk at my butler. Elise left late that morning, and it was barely past noon before another visitor came knocking. At this rate, I would never get anything done. "Send him in."

Cauldron walked in the door a moment later, his eyes bloodshot like he hadn't slept in a couple days. He dropped onto one of the couches without saying a word to me.

He looked like shit, but it would be wrong to kick him when he was already down. "What happened?"

He leaned back in the cushions and put his feet on my coffee table.

I let his lack of manners slide.

I came around the desk and sat across from him. "Scotch?"

He raised his hand and shook it. "If I have any more, I'll drop dead."

"That doesn't sound good."

His neck rested on the back of the cushion, and he looked at the ceiling for a while. "I fucked up, man."

"You don't say."

"I went to her apartment...and it's like she hates me."

"I don't mean to make you feel bad, Cauldron, but you hurt her pretty bad. And more than once."

He straightened in the chair, forearms moving to his knees. "She's back in the business. Bartholomew is her client."

That was disappointing news. She'd dreamed of getting out of the business to do something else with her life, but she wound up back in the same place. And Bartholomew wasn't a regular client. He lived a dangerous life.

"She said she likes him."

"I'm sorry." They were hollow words, but it was better than saying nothing at all.

"I tried to get her back, but she said no."

"Why would you do that?"

His eyes moved to mine.

"Nothing has changed. She knows that. So why would she say yes?"

"Everything has changed. It's been the worst month of my life."

"I suspect she agrees with me on this. Seems like you only want her out of jealousy."

He gave me a cold look. "It certainly helps... I'll give you that."

"She's given you plenty of chances, Cauldron. She'd have no self-respect if she did it again—"

"Whose side are you on, exactly?"

"I know her better than you do. That's all."

He sank back into the couch. "I've never seen her like that. Never seen her possess such indifference mixed with rage. I felt like a goddamn stranger. An inconvenience to her life."

I turned quiet and let him vent his frustrations.

"But when I told her I hadn't been with anyone else... she gave me this look. She couldn't hide it as hard as she tried. It was quick and faint, but I caught it."

"Meaning?"

"She still loves me."

"I don't think loving you is the issue, Cauldron. It's trust—and she doesn't have that."

"I think as long as those feelings are there, there's a chance."

I gave a loud sigh because this was a fruitless endeavor. "I don't think you can put any set of words together to convince her to go down that road again. Besides, the contract she's under is ironclad. I nearly had to kill Kyle to get him to back down."

"Didn't you sublease a contract to be with Elise?"

My eyes narrowed. "Yes. Technically."

"What if I did the same with Bartholomew?"

Was he saying what I thought he was saying? "You're going to buy him off?"

"Yes."

I stared at the floor for a minute as I considered the proposal. "That could backfire."

"The worst he could say is no."

"And you'll accept that answer?" I asked in disbelief.

"Everything has a price."

"Even if this plan works, doesn't mean she'll cooperate. If she likes him, she'll probably be pissed."

Cauldron gave a shrug. "She wanted back in the business. This is how business works."

"What about Roan? He's in town."

"We can do both."

"Can we?" I asked. "Because all you seem to care about is Camille."

"Have they made a hit on you? No. So, calm down."

I spoke through gritted teeth. "I am calm, asshole."

He relaxed against the couch, turning quiet as he remained lost in thought.

I reached for my glass and took a drink.

"You think you could talk to her?"

Good thing I'd just swallowed. Otherwise, I would have spit it all out. "Me?"

"You two are obviously friends…or something."

Or something was more accurate.

"She stayed with you for two weeks. You bought her an apartment. An apartment I'm going to pay you back for."

"It was a gift."

"She's my woman."

"She saved my life, so it's a gift." I wouldn't take his money. Or her money.

Cauldron sidestepped the subject. "Will you talk to her?"

"And say what, exactly?"

"That she should give me another chance."

I stared at my brother, feeling conflicted.

Cauldron studied my gaze, saw my unspoken thoughts. "You won't do it."

"I can't. I'm sorry."

His face went pale, as if I'd stabbed him in the back and drained his blood. "Why?"

"I don't want to get involved—"

"Bullshit. That's not the reason."

"You really want me to say it?" I asked incredulously. "I don't think you've changed. I don't think anything is different. I'm not going to convince her to put herself in the same situation that nearly broke her. She and I are done, but that doesn't mean I don't still care about her."

Cauldron looked away, his face still white as snow.

"I'm sorry, man."

"I don't think I'd be this miserable if things hadn't changed. I wouldn't be willing to pay off Bartholomew if I wasn't serious."

I kept my mouth shut.

"What could I do to prove otherwise?"

I still didn't say anything.

"Grave?"

"I'm not going to answer that."

"Why?"

"Because if things were truly different, you would know."

20

CAULDRON

"This is a bad idea." Grave stood beside me on the dark sidewalk near the bridge, his breath so thick it looked like smoke from a cigar. "You're walking into their lair without invitation."

"He'll respect me more because of it."

"Or he'll kill you."

"I'm not asking you to come with me, Grave." I didn't ask him to drive there with me either. I could handle this on my own, but he insisted on joining.

"We know he does business with Roan."

"I don't see how that's relevant."

"It's relevant because he'll know we're no longer estranged if I show my face."

"Then stay here."

Grave wore that irritated look, like I'd just asked him to do the impossible.

"I've survived worse." I walked on, headed down the hill to the hidden location.

"If you aren't back within the hour, I'm coming after you."

I kept going, making my way down to the bottom of the bridge until I reached the entrance. There were no guards, not when anyone stationed outside would make the area look conspicuous. I moved through the dark pipe for nearly five minutes before I reached the bedrock.

Then I saw the glow of torches. I saw the colored limestone, the skulls that had been part of the foundation for hundreds of years. The air was immediately stale and dank, like it hadn't moved in a thousand years. I turned down the tunnel, coming face-to-face with one of the men stationed at the entrance.

With a cold look, he sized me up.

"I'm here for Bartholomew."

"Bartholomew has no standing appointments."

"I just want to talk to him."

"So do a lot of people. Get out."

"Tell him it's about Camille. Trust me, he'll want to see me then."

He sized me up again. "Who the fuck are you?"

"Cauldron Beaufort." I would have called him, but his information was impossible to track down. He was a well-known player in Paris, but he was constantly elusive, untouchable.

"Stay here." He rounded the corner of the tunnel and disappeared.

I stayed there, breathing in the underground musk, listening to the random echoes that traveled through the tunnels. Sound carried through the air like a wired microphone. I could hear the conversation between two men who were nowhere near me.

The guy finally returned fifteen minutes later. He gave a nod for me to follow him.

We moved through the tunnels, guided by the lit torches. Nooks in the walls showed piles of skulls, untouched for several lifetimes. The Catacombs underneath the streets of Paris were once open to the public, but Bartholomew managed to strike a deal with men in high places to claim it as his. The Parisian government was aware of its criminal purposes, but they looked the other way because the price was right. It was impressive because most criminals had to operate in the shadows.

The cavern started to open, and I found myself in an enormous room that housed hundreds of men, all sitting at tables drinking ale out of tankards. They all looked at me, all armed, their eyes like bullets.

I'd left my gun in the car, but I should have brought it since they didn't check me. I doubted it was due to negligence. More like arrogance.

At the rear of the cavern was a throne made out of skulls. It seemed to have been cut from the wall and filed down into a chair. It didn't look comfortable, but that didn't stop Bartholomew from looking comfortable as he sat there, knees far apart, his arms on the armrests, his hands gripping the skulls at the very ends. He was in a black leather jacket and black jeans. His boots were military grade, the leather shiny. His dark eyes were pinpointed on me, watching me with a blank stare.

The room fell quiet, all the men ending their conversations to watch the exchange.

I approached the throne, seeing his face follow me the entire way. He didn't blink. Just evaluated me with a stare that reminded me of the skulls he sat on. This place was more than a criminal organization. It was a cult.

I stopped in front of him, a bit annoyed this conversation would have so many witnesses.

Bartholomew kept up that indifferent gaze, maintaining the power by refusing to speak first.

"Can we speak in private?"

"You come to my home and make demands?" His voice was quiet and slightly restrained. "I may sit upon the throne, but we're all one and the same. What you confide to me can be confided to those who surround you."

A fucking cult. "Even if it pertains to your personal life?"

His eyes narrowed slightly. "Make your request and leave."

Camille liked this guy? "I want to sublease the remainder of your contract with Camille."

He was still as the stone that surrounded him, having no discernible reaction. "She doesn't seem to like you very much."

"It's complicated."

"Women aren't complicated. Be honest with your intentions. Keep your word. Don't fuck someone else. That's all they want. Which means you violated one of those three rules."

I had to keep the comeback locked tightly behind my jaw.

"Which one was it?" He tilted his head slightly, his eyes still wide open because he hadn't blinked yet. "I don't think you fucked someone else. Not when Camille is utterly stunning. No, that's not it..."

This guy was fucking infuriating.

"Are you a liar? Men like us don't like...so that's probably not it." His fingers brushed over the shadow of his jawline. "Which means you weren't honest with your intentions. Yes...that sounds about right. You told her you wanted more—until you didn't."

I suspected Camille had confided all of this to him, and now he was fucking with me. "What's your price?"

"I don't have one."

"Then I'll go first. Three million."

He finally blinked, and when he did, he possessed a bored look. "I don't have a price because she's not for sale."

Shit. "Five million."

His fingers curled under his jaw, and he stared.

"Ten."

He didn't move. Now he blended into the throne.

"Fifteen."

He didn't seem remotely enticed.

"How about fifty?" No way he would say no to that. Fifty million dollars for nothing.

"As I already said, she's not for sale. But please, continue listing off random numbers that don't impress me."

Fucking prick. "There must be something you want more than her."

"She's indispensable."

What the fuck?

His hand returned to the skull at the edge of the armrest. "Our business has concluded."

I couldn't walk away. I couldn't sleep knowing this asshole was balls deep in my girl every night. He refused to sell her, and she liked him, and that meant it could get serious if I didn't intervene. "Bartholomew, there has to be something I can do—"

"Leave." Now his voice turned sinister, like the beast inside him had stirred. "I kindly listened to your request. I gave you an inch—don't you dare ask for a mile. Leave now, and we part on good terms. Overstay your welcome, and you'll be another skull upon this chair."

It was raining.

Soaked to the bone, we stepped into the bar.

The bartender looked at us in disapproval but didn't dare voice it.

Grave and I took a seat on the leather stools, our clothes heavy from being drenched. The scotch was poured and placed in front of us, and I slouched against the counter, utterly defeated.

"At least he didn't kill you."

"I wish I were dead..." I threw my head back and took a drink.

"Did he ask for too much?"

"He said she wasn't for sale—for any price. I offered him fifty million, and he didn't blink an eye over it. He said she's indispensable...whatever the fuck that means. The guy's a fucking prick too."

"Why's he a prick?"

"He just is." I took another drink.

"You tried."

"And I'll try again."

Grave turned to me, alarm on his face. "Don't kick the hornet's nest."

"There has to be something he wants."

"You already asked."

I slammed the glass down. "There has to be *something*."

Grave pried the empty glass from my fingertips before I could shatter it. He pushed it forward so the bartender could refill it. "He's in business with Roan, but that doesn't mean anything. They could be allies or enemies."

"What does that mean?"

"I know Bartholomew is an ambitious guy. Maybe he hands off his supplies to Roan to sell in Croatia. Or maybe he wants to eliminate Roan so he can sell directly in Croatia. There's no way to know unless we ask. But the second you ask…"

"I'm showing my hand." And that could be deadly.

"I don't need to tell you it's a bad idea."

"I'm desperate."

"Even if this works, that doesn't mean Camille will cooperate."

"She'll have to cooperate."

The bartender refilled the glass, and I brought it back to my lips where it belonged. "Two birds, one stone. We need to kill Roan anyway."

"If that's what Bartholomew wants…"

"I can always convince him to want it. Tell him to scale his business. Claim all of Europe instead of such a small part of it."

"Maybe," Grave said.

"I know that's what he wants. I can tell by the way he looks, by the way he talks."

"We've got one problem. How are you going to talk to him again? You can't walk back in there."

"Just watch Camille. She'll lead us to him."

The black SUV pulled up to the apartment.

"Here we go." I inhaled a deep breath as I waited for Bartholomew to exit the vehicle and walk to the front door. Nothing happened. The SUV remained idle, exhaust leaking out of the pipe.

Minutes later, the front door opened and revealed a strip of light down the stairs and pavement. Camille appeared, in a rose-pink dress that showed her bare skin on either side of her belly button. It was a cocktail dress, but playful in color. It looked great on her, and for a moment, my gaze was transfixed.

Then she got into the back seat and disappeared.

The SUV drove right past us, and I looked straight ahead to appear less obvious.

"I don't think Bartholomew is in the back," Grave said.

"No. I think his guy is taking her to him." I made a U-turn in the middle of the road and allowed a car between the SUV and me so it would be less obvious I was tailing him. After several intersections and a couple of turns, we pulled up to one of the lesser-known art museums in Paris. There were people outside in tuxedos and gowns. "Cocktail party." Camille was already out of the car and walking up the stairs—alone.

"We gotta change first."

We parked on a different street and fished our tuxedos out of the trunk. Once we looked our finest, we walked up the steps and through the entryway. We didn't have invitations and we weren't on the list, but thankfully they recognized Grave and assumed his missing name was just an accident.

It was a silent auction. The paintings were on display in the main room as well as in smaller adjacent rooms. People wrote down their bids on a folded piece of paper and dropped it into the lockbox, so no one knew what others had bid. It was more than a silent auction, but a mystery auction. Grave and I felt out of place walking in there together and without dates, but hope-fully people wouldn't notice.

"So, what's the plan here?" Grave asked as he took a drink off the tray. "The second she sees you, you're in trouble."

My eyes moved across the room, catching sight of the pink dress. She stood beside Bartholomew, drink in hand, and together, they examined a painting without touching each other. His head was slightly turned to her as he spoke, but I couldn't read his lips.

"You think he told her about last night?" Grave asked.

I was thankful Bartholomew's arm wasn't secured around her waist. If it were, I would lose my shit. "No."

"Why not?"

"He's not much of a talker." I had barely a sip of my champagne before I returned it to a passing tray. "You need to pull her away."

"Me?" he asked, slightly incredulous.

"Why do you think you're here?"

"To do business. Not babysit."

"Unless we wait all night for her to go to the bathroom, she's going to see us."

"How am I supposed to get her attention without him seeing me?"

I looked at the waitresses walking around, and a thought struck me. I grabbed a paper from the bidding table and scribbled the message before I handed it to the waitress along with a generous tip. "Give this to the woman in the pink dress." When she walked away, I turned to Grave. "Wait for her outside the bathroom. Now."

Grave gave an annoyed sigh. "This is far below my pay grade..." He walked off to meet her.

I watched Camille open the note and discreetly read it.

Bartholomew seemed too absorbed in the painting to notice. Or he just didn't care.

Camille took the bait and walked off to the bathroom.

Showtime.

Bartholomew scribbled his bid for one of the paintings before he dropped the paper into the box.

I appeared at his side. "Where are you going to put it?"

He had no reaction at all, like he knew I was there the whole time or he was just that calm and collected. "In my study."

He ran an all-cash business. What did he need a study for?

"You think I won't pull out my knife just because this room is full of people?" He lifted his glass and took another drink, sliding his hand into his pocket like he was reaching for his blade. He pivoted his body, looking at me head on. "Because I will."

"I have something you might want."

The corner of his mouth quirked up in a slightly amused smile. "You got it bad, huh?"

"You turned down fifty million—so you got it bad too."

He continued to look amused. "Cauldron, you like games?"

My eyes shifted back and forth between his.

"Because I do. You want to play?"

I suspected I didn't have a choice.

"Here's how it goes. Present your business proposition, and if I don't like it, I cut your throat where you stand. If I do like it, the blade stays in my pocket. But there's another option." He held up his glass a little higher. "Walk away now, and we don't play at all. What do you say?"

After a long standoff, I made my decision. "I'll take my chances."

"Ah." He set the glass on an empty tray of a passing waiter. "I was hoping you'd say that." Now both hands were in his pockets, one set of fingers no doubt gripping the handle of his concealed blade. "Go ahead."

"Roan is your distributor to Croatia and Eastern Europe. He's taking the risk by getting the drugs across the border, but he's taking a big cut. Based on my information, he's selling your stuff for three times what you sell it for here."

I knew I had his attention when he cocked his head slightly, and his eyes narrowed like a sharper lens on a telescope.

"If Roan were removed, you could sell directly. Take over his distribution network and keep all the profits for yourself. Word on the street is you have your eyes set on Italy, so I know you're looking to expand."

Bartholomew's eyes were so sharp, they were like the blade in his pocket. "Business advice? That's all you have to offer me."

"I'll kill him for you."

He didn't blink. Didn't take a breath. "You think I can't kill a man myself?"

"I'm giving you plausible deniability. If people knew you stabbed your partner in the back, no one would ever want to do business with you. I'll take care of Roan—and you give me Camille." I laid it all out on the table. No going back.

Bartholomew stared and stared, as if I hadn't said a word.

I kept my patience, letting him think this through. Since the knife stayed in his pocket, I assumed my throat was safe for now.

"You kill Roan, and I'll let you sublease my contract."

I did it. I fucking did it. "We have a deal—"

"For fifty million."

It was greedy, but I wasn't going to negotiate and push my luck. He could keep the money. "Deal."

He slid his right hand out of his pocket.

My eyes immediately glanced down to make sure the knife wasn't there.

He gave a slight smile. "Other hand." He reached his right hand forward to shake mine.

I took it.

"You can have her starting tomorrow."

"*Tonight.*" He didn't get to go home and fuck her one last time.

"I need her for this event. Once we're finished, she can go."

What did he need her for?

"Besides, no money, no deal. You'll need an hour or two to gather that amount of cash. Drop it off at the Catacombs. Once every bill is accounted for and my men confirm it's not counterfeit, they'll let me know the deal is done."

"You drop her off at home and leave. That's it."

Now he looked amused again. "I might give her a good-night kiss. But then, she's all yours."

21

CAMILLE

"What the fuck are you doing here?" I hissed once we were outside the bathroom.

Grave was in his tuxedo, his built frame filling out the material well. He stared at me for a while, visibly flustered as he considered what to say. "Cauldron told me about your conversation. I thought we should talk about it."

"*Now?*"

"I came here to meet a client, and I spotted you across the room. You know Bartholomew is dangerous, right?"

"And you aren't?" I asked incredulously. "He's never kept me as a prisoner. And he's never drawn a gun on me and pulled the trigger. So he's definitely less dangerous than you and your brother."

"Wait, Cauldron shot you?"

"The chamber was empty... It's a long story."

His eyes were still narrowed in shock.

"Just stay out of my business, Grave."

"I don't think you understand what you're getting yourself into—"

"My life. My choice."

"What happened to settling down and having a family?"

"I'd still love that, but there's just one problem. All men are fucking pigs." I turned to storm off.

He grabbed me by the wrist and yanked me back. "I'm not telling you to get back together with Cauldron. But this sure as hell isn't the answer. You're better than this."

"*Better than this*? Does that mean Elise is *better than this*?"

With his fingers still locked around my wrist, he stared me down.

I twisted out of his grasp, and he let me go. "Stay out of my business—"

"Do you still love Cauldron?"

The question had me taken aback.

"I think you do. And I don't know how you can screw someone if you're in love with someone else."

I stared.

He stared back.

Both of us were fuming.

And then I walked away. "Fuck off, Grave."

I returned to Bartholomew's side, trying to look as normal as possible.

He'd just scribbled a bid on a piece of paper and dropped it inside.

"Nice painting."

He gave a shrug and continued to the next piece.

"Why did you bid, then?"

"That's what you do, right?" He stopped in front of the next one. "What do you think about this?"

I looked at the bright colors of the garden, the pastel hues of the flowers. "It's pretty."

"Looks like it belongs in a bathroom." He moved on to the next one.

"So...what's the plan for tonight?"

"Straight down to business, I see. If I didn't know any better, I'd say you enjoy this line of work."

"I guess it is a bit thrilling..."

"Well, that's too bad..."

"What's too bad?"

He stared at the next painting, hands resting in his pockets.

I waited for an answer. "What's too bad?" I repeated.

Again, he ignored me.

———

At the end of the night, Bartholomew took me home.

On the drive, he got a phone call. Whenever he answered the phone, he didn't say anything, just listened to the silence on the other end. After a few seconds, he said, "It's all there? Good." He hung up.

These sorts of calls happened all the time. I was used to them.

We pulled up to my apartment, and Bartholomew walked me to the front door. For a man so dangerous, he had the manners of a gentleman. Breath escaped his nostrils like vapor, and he stood on the threshold with his hands concealed in his pockets.

I got the door unlocked. "I guess I'll see you later."

He remained in place, staring.

I knew he had something to say. He just needed to decide when to say it.

"Our business relationship has concluded."

First, it was shock. Then it was panic. "But our contract hasn't expired…"

"I've agreed to sublease it."

"Sublease? What does that mean?"

"Someone purchased the remainder of your contract for a generous fee."

"What…?"

He leaned against the wall and crossed his ankles.

I didn't want anyone else. I wanted Bartholomew. "You—you did this without asking me."

"For what it's worth, I said no at first. But the guy wouldn't let up."

"Who's the guy?"

Silence.

"I said, who's the guy?"

He gave me a hard stare. "You know who it is."

Cauldron. "No..."

"I'm sorry. He gave me an offer I couldn't refuse."

"But I don't want him. I want you."

A half smile moved on to his lips. "Wow, I think I'm blushing."

"Undo it. Please."

"I've already accepted the money."

"Aren't you a billionaire?" My voice became shrill as the panic took over. "What do you need money for?"

"He offered me something besides money."

"What?"

He gave a slight shrug. "It wouldn't interest you."

"Tell me."

"Well, he offered to kill someone for me."

"You can't do your own dirty work?" I asked with a raised eyebrow.

He released a slight chuckle. "You really hate this guy, don't you?"

"Don't this to me, Bartholomew. I'm begging you..."

"I'm sorry, Camille. The deal is done."

I almost fell to my knees right then and there. I was literally back to where I started.

"If it makes you feel any better, it'll be hard to replace you."

"I doubt that." When I remembered Grave at the museum, it suddenly clicked in my head. That was all just a distraction. Grave kept me busy while Cauldron made his move. We'd been in the same room together, and I didn't even know. "I can't believe this is happening."

Bartholomew stared at me for a while longer, his eyes slightly sympathetic. "Take care, Camille."

I released a painful sigh.

"It was nothing personal." He gave me a slight nod before he walked to the SUV parked at the curb. He got inside and drove away, and once he was gone, I knew my life had changed. Just when I thought I'd made progress toward a different future, I was ripped straight back into the past.

I knew Cauldron could show up at any moment.

I didn't bother taking off my dress.

I sat on the couch with a glass of wine in hand, knowing a knock would sound on my door at some point. A little buzz would make the conversation more bearable. The night deepened to some unearthly hour, and my stomach gave a quiet rumble because I'd skipped dinner.

Then I heard it.

Knock. Knock. Knock.

"Shit…" I remained seated, staring into the hallway that led to the front door. I could ignore him, but that would only last for a minute or two. He'd break down the door or come at me some other time. There was no escaping this.

Knock. Knock. Knock. It was louder this time, filled with impatience.

I left the wine behind and headed to the front door. Without checking the peephole, I opened it, coming face-to-face with the man I didn't want to see. In jeans and a long-sleeved shirt, he stared at me with his arms by his sides. His eyes flicked back and forth between mine as he studied my reaction, as if there was a chance Bartholomew hadn't told me that I'd changed hands like a goddamn horse.

Now he knew.

"You may have bought me out, but I'm not your whore. If you think I'm going to get on my back for you, you're going to be sorely disappointed."

His eyes continued to examine mine in silence. There was no rebuttal.

"You got that?"

"I'll pick you up tomorrow at seven."

"Excuse me? For what?"

"Dinner." He turned around and took the stairs.

"Not happening. You don't own me, Cauldron."

He stopped on the bottom step and slowly turned around.

I held my ground and stared him down.

"Actually, I do own you. I own you until the conclusion of your contract. If you wanted to keep your rights, you shouldn't have sold yourself to Jerome. You shouldn't have walked into that bar and put yourself at the mercy of men like me." He walked back up the steps, taking his time until he was right in front of me again. "You made your bed. Now lie in it."

"This is bullshit."

Jerome sat in his chair and gave a slight shrug. "I'm sorry, Camille."

"This can't be right. He can't do that."

"Grave did the same with Elise. Subleases happen."

"But it was without my knowledge."

He gave another shrug. "The guy who owns the contract can do whatever he wants."

"I'm a fucking person."

He just stared at me.

"There's gotta be a way out of this."

He shook his head.

"I won't do it. Get me another client."

"I can't, Camille."

"Why the hell not?"

"Because Bartholomew is still paying his fee, which means you're unavailable."

"He doesn't have to know anything."

"I'm not stupid enough to take on both Bartholomew and Cauldron. And no one is going to want to buy a contract when they know you've already got a contract and a sublease with two powerful men. You're stuck."

I slumped in the chair, devastated. "This can't be happening."

"I'm sorry."

"I didn't agree to this."

"Doesn't matter. You should have read the fine print before you signed the contract."

Shame on me.

"Do your time. Make the best of it."

"Make the *best* of it?" I snapped. "I don't think that's possible."

22

CAMILLE

He knocked on the door—at seven o'clock sharp.

"Here we go..." There was no escaping these two men. I was either at the mercy of Grave or at the mercy of Cauldron. Depending on the day of the week, it could change. I assumed we were going somewhere fancy, so I'd put on a black cocktail dress with pumps with a sharp point, you know, in case I needed to kick him in the balls.

I opened the door, seeing him standing in his signature long-sleeved shirt and dark jeans.

His eyes were locked on mine, and they looked empty down to their core. When he'd come to my home to talk to me about Bartholomew, he'd worn his heart on his sleeve, showed a side of himself that hardly existed, but that was long gone now. He was back to his former coldness. Now that he owed me, he didn't have to be nice, didn't have to say a word to me. "You look beautiful."

"Really? I thought I looked angry."

"I've always thought you look beautiful when you're angry." A slight smile tugged at the corner of his lips.

I marched past him to the car. "Let's get this over with."

He drove to the restaurant and tossed the keys to the valet before we headed inside. A table was waiting for him, a lone white candle in the center. The wine was poured, and the bread was placed between us.

Then we were alone together.

I couldn't believe I was there, across from Cauldron, like our lives hadn't changed.

He opened his menu and looked at the selections.

I just stared at him, wanting to dig the butter knife into the back of his palm.

"What are you having?" he asked, his eyes down.

"Something with lots of garlic and onions..."

A subtle laugh escaped his lips as he continued to read. "Not enough garlic and onions in the world, baby."

"Don't call me that."

His eyes lifted, his smile gone. "I can call you whatever I want." He held my gaze for a moment before he looked at the menu again.

"Assholes..."

He acted like he didn't hear me.

I browsed the menu but didn't crave anything since I had no appetite.

When the waitress came over to take our order, I decided on a salad. He got the steak—typical.

Then we sat there in silence. Heavy silence. Uncomfortable silence. He stared at me with one arm resting on the table, looking at me the way he used to, during better times, when I'd pictured the two of us together forever. I wished I could see my own expression because it was probably ice-cold.

It didn't deter him. "How are you liking your apartment?"

I ignored the question.

"I noticed your fireplace. It's nice."

I looked away and pretended he didn't exist entirely.

"Would you prefer to spend the evening in complete silence?"

My eyes shifted back to him.

"Because that's not going to change anything. You can ignore me and eat all the onions and garlic you want... won't change anything."

Last night, I'd been at a gallery auction with Bartholomew, actually being useful in ways beyond sex. And now, I was stuck here...with a man who'd broken my heart. "Remember when you pulled that gun on me and pulled the trigger?"

He stayed quiet.

"That's when I should have known."

"Known what?" he asked quietly.

"That you were truly heartless."

"You think I'm heartless? Bartholomew's worse."

I shook my head. "I thoroughly enjoyed his company. I wish I were with him now instead of you."

Cauldron tried to keep a straight face, but there was a subtle flicker of pain...or anger. Not sure which. "You don't know him as well as you think."

"I know him as a man. I know how he treats a woman —and he's a perfect gentleman."

"Are we talking about the same guy?" he asked, slightly raising his voice. "The guy who threatened to slice my throat open in a room full of people if I didn't win his little game? The guy who digs up corpses just to smuggle his drugs across the border? The guy who wears military boots so he can execute his enemies by stomping on their skulls until they break? That guy? You should be thanking me for getting you out of that situation."

"You can say what you want about him, but he keeps his word, is honest about his intentions, and doesn't stick his dick in other women. Which is a lot more than you can say about yourself."

"I never fucked anyone else. Still haven't."

"But you're a liar. A big, fat liar. You were dishonest about our relationship from the beginning. And then you were dishonest again after I forgave you."

"I told you I tried—"

"It doesn't matter. Say what you want about Bartholomew, but what you see is what you get."

The redness in his face showed a hint of the anger underneath. Every time Bartholomew's name was said, it got a little bit worse.

Good.

"I need to see him."

"Well, he's in the middle of a meeting," his butler said in the parlor. "It'll have to wait."

I was tempted to storm right past him and enter the office anyway, but that would be pretty rude after Grave had bought me that apartment. I let out a frustrated sigh and took a seat on one of the stiff couches. It was still January, so the sky was always overcast, and there was always a frost against the windows that fogged the view.

Thirty minutes later, footsteps sounded down the hallway before they entered the parlor. First, it was Grave, wearing his signature sweatpants without a shirt, because he chose to conduct his business as casually as possible. And then behind him came Cauldron.

Cauldron stopped and stared at me, a steely gaze that lacked any sign of affection. He must have still been angry about the night before because his expression was identical to how it was then. It must have remained on his face, permanent.

I held his stare without moving. Time seemed to stand still.

Then he walked off without saying a word to Grave. He disappeared into the elevator and then was gone.

Grave sat on the other couch. "That was rough."

"If you think that was rough, you should have joined us for dinner last night."

"Did you need something?"

"You really can't guess why I'm here?" I asked incredulously. "You thought your little distraction at the art auction would go unnoticed?"

He stared at me, giving no admission of guilt.

"I can't believe you helped him."

"He's my brother. It's not that hard to believe."

"But I'm your—" I couldn't find the right word because I really wasn't sure what we were these days. "Friend..."

"I understand why you won't give Cauldron another chance, but Bartholomew is not the answer. You never should have gotten back in the game. You're the first one to admit that it's gotten you in the worst kind of trouble."

I rolled my eyes. "You don't know him."

"I know him better than you—"

"Well, you don't know him the way *I* know him."

Silence passed. He massaged his knuckles. "Were you in love with him or something?"

"No."

"Was that where it was headed?"

"I don't have to answer your questions. It was fucked up that you interfered and got me stuck with Cauldron again. After everything he put me through, how could you want me with him again? You know better than anyone how much he hurt me."

He said nothing.

"Just because he's your brother? That's a terrible reason to push me on him."

"I never said I wanted you back with him. In fact, he asked me to convince you to give him another chance, and I said no."

Now I was the one who turned silent.

"I said no because he's fucked up too many times, and I'm not convinced that he's really changed. Just wants what he can't have."

"That's what you think?"

He gave a shrug. "I'm not sure. But you've been his guinea pig long enough."

My eyes dropped momentarily, unexpectedly hurt by his confession.

"But that didn't stop him from pursuing you, so maybe I'm wrong."

I looked at him again.

"You want me to be wrong." It was somewhat of a question, somewhat of a realization.

"I guess...but I know you aren't."

A knock sounded on my door.

I was in the kitchen cooking dinner, making a salad with grilled chicken and French dressing. I turned off the stove then walked to the peephole, my heart giving a jolt of adrenaline when I recognized Cauldron's face on the other side. "Bastard..."

"I heard that."

I unlocked the door and opened it. "Good."

He was dressed casually tonight, like he had no plans to whisk me away to a fancy restaurant that wouldn't impress me. He was in a long-sleeved shirt and dark jeans with boots, the cold air escaping his nostrils as icy vapor.

"What?"

"I'd like to come in."

"I don't remember inviting you."

"I don't have to be invited."

I thought my iciness the other night would have driven him away, but it had only bought me a small amount of time.

"I paid for that luxury."

I stepped away from the open door and returned to the kitchen. "I was making dinner. Do you want any?"

"Yes." He shut the door and locked it behind him.

Presumptuous...but whatever.

I dished up two servings and placed them on the dining table.

He took a look around as he came into the room. "You got more furniture."

"Yes. Just taken awhile for everything to come in."

He took the seat across from me, and we ate in silence. My eyes were down on my food the entire time, but I could tell he was staring at me. I was in a loose sweatshirt with leggings, my makeup gone because I hadn't left the apartment all day. It was one of those days when I felt like doing nothing.

"What were you and Grave talking about?" When I looked up, he'd eaten all of his food, and now he was just staring at me.

"Business."

"What kind of business?"

"I have to kill someone tomorrow."

Now that the conversation turned serious, I lost my appetite. "Why do you have to kill him?"

"If I don't, he'll kill Grave. We're doing it together."

I gave a slight nod in understanding. "This is the guy with the drugs?"

"Yes."

"Bartholomew is in the same line of work...maybe he could help."

"Actually, that was the price I paid for you."

My blood suddenly went cold.

"He didn't accept any monetary offer that I made. But he accepted that one. With Roan out of the way, he'll be able to expand his distribution and take over new territory."

"So, if you die...it's my fault."

With his arms on the table, he stared at me. "It's my fault because I was the one who let you go. It's my fault because I ruined the best thing that ever happened to me. It's my fault—and mine alone."

All of that made me uneasy. I might hate Cauldron right now, but I certainly didn't want him to die. "Do you have a plan? A good one?"

"Yes."

I gave a slight nod. "Grave is going to help you?"

"Yes."

That made me feel better, but it also made me feel worse. I wondered if Elise knew about this.

"I'll be alright, baby."

I wanted to lash out and tell him to shut his mouth, but I had no control over the things he said and did anymore. I gathered the dishes and set them in the sink. I assumed he would leave now, so I walked to the front door and quickly realized he had no intention of following me. When I returned to the sitting room, he was on one of the couches, comfortable, like he intended to stay awhile.

I crossed my arms over my chest, self-conscious in the baggy clothes. "I'm not prepared to entertain."

"You don't need to entertain me." He sat with one arm on the armrest, his knees wide apart, covering one end of my couch with his size.

"I was just going to read."

"Then read."

I continued to stand there, holding his gaze with unease. "Cauldron, I'm not going to sleep with you. You should just go."

He cocked his head slightly, his eyes giving a small reaction. "You think that's my endgame?"

"That's what you paid for, isn't it?"

"I paid for *you*. In any capacity that you're willing to give me."

"I'm not willing to give you *anything*. You're forcing me to."

It turned into a silent standoff. His eyes darkened. "You don't want me here, but you seem terrified of losing me."

"Just because I don't want to be with you doesn't mean I want you dead, Cauldron."

"But you want Bartholomew?" Now his voice changed, turning as angry as his face looked at our dinner a few nights ago.

"Yes. I enjoyed his company."

It was the coldest look he'd ever given me. Fierce in its intensity. Just as terrifying as the loaded barrel of a gun. "You can replace me that easily?" His voice was quiet, but both deadly and broken. "I'm the one who ended things, but I could never, ever imagine myself with anyone else, at least not this soon, even if it meant nothing to me—because you mean everything to me."

His words actually hurt me. Hurt me because I could see how much I hurt him. I thought it would make me feel good, but it made me feel like shit. Made me feel like I was the one in the wrong. But I held my silence and didn't reveal a single truth because this was the best way to get him out of my life.

It was the best way to make sure he didn't hurt me again.

After an endless stare, he got to his feet and walked out the door.

It worked...

23

CAULDRON

After a thorough pat-down and several different kinds of security checks for explosives and bombs, I was permitted into his residence. It was a large estate in the city, an apartment closed off by an iron gate with no access to the public.

I was escorted inside, to the third floor, where I found Bartholomew waiting for me on the couch near the fire, shirtless and in his black sweatpants, like he'd retired for the evening. His build was like mine, slender and ripped, only muscle underneath the skin. There was a scar on his stomach, like someone had shot him and made their mark.

"It was a misunderstanding." He answered the question I never asked. One elbow propped on the armrest, and his knees were wide apart. The coffee table held a collection of booze, practically a wet bar, but he didn't seem to be drinking.

I sat on the couch across from him.

"You should be balls deep in your new investment."

If only. "She's not interested."

"You've given her a choice. What a gentleman." His fingers curled into a fist, and he propped his chin on top of them, just the way he sat on his throne in the Catacombs. He stared me down and waited for me to explain my presence.

"She hates me."

"You didn't know that before? You should always do your research prior to a big purchase."

I wanted to punch him in the face.

"Oh, that's right. You *did* know. Because I told you."

Fucking cunt.

"You made a deal, Cauldron. You have to see it through."

"I'll take care of Roan tomorrow. But she wants you —not me."

One of his eyebrows cocked slightly. "Is that so?"

"You're really going to rub it in my face?"

"My curiosity is genuine."

This was torture. "She prefers you as a client over me. She's said it many, many times. I can't listen to her say it again. I'll shoot myself between the eyes."

Bartholomew fell into silence, his intelligent eyes seeming to be elsewhere. "Interesting. I think Camille has a taste for the criminal underworld. She was nervous at first, but then she really embraced it."

My eyes narrowed. "What the fuck are you talking about?"

"I used to put her to work. Distract men so I could get access to a corridor. Talk to one of the wives so I could do business with her husband. Sometimes things more extensive...if she was up for it."

"So, she was your wingman?"

"Essentially."

"And you... Did you two ever..." I couldn't bring myself to actually ask the question.

He gave a slight smile. "I'm not the kind of man to kiss-and-tell, Cauldron. Or should I say fuck-and-gloat?"

It was like someone smashed a rock right into my heart.

"But good thing for you, there was no kissing and fucking. Well, that's not entirely true..." He scratched his beard with his fingertips. "There was one kiss. A kiss that she turned down...because she was in love with some other guy." He used his thumb and forefinger to mimic a gun and point it at me. "Something tells me you're that guy."

Grave checked the screen of his phone. "It's Camille."

I looked out the window of the car, staring at the building we were about to infiltrate.

"Why the fuck is she calling me right now?" With gritted teeth, he took the call. "I'm kinda in the middle of something right now—"

"I know." Her voice could be heard in the quiet car. "Cauldron said you guys were going to get some guy tonight."

Grave waited for her to say something more, but nothing was forthcoming. "So you decided to call me in the middle of it?"

"I just wanted to know your plan."

"Why?" he barked. "What does it matter to you?"

"Because I don't want you guys to get killed, maybe?" she snapped. "Can I help?"

"No," Grave said in a bored voice. "You can't help, Camille."

"I've learned a couple things with Bartholomew, so maybe I can lend you a hand."

Grave's eyebrows furrowed. "What the fuck are you talking about?"

"It's a long story—"

"Camille, I've got to go."

"Wait." Now her voice softened. "Is Cauldron with you?"

"He's right next to me."

Silence.

My eyes stayed on the building, but I could imagine her right next to me, that fear in her bright eyes, a subtle film of moisture that reflected the lights from the dashboard.

"Why?" Grave asked.

"I-I just want you guys to be safe. Be careful."

"You want to tell him that yourself?" Grave looked at me, the phone held to his ear.

Silence.

She spoke again. "No. Just...please be careful. Let me know when it's done." She hung up.

Grave sighed and slipped the phone into his pocket. "Sounds like your plan hasn't worked too well..."

"Not really. She doesn't talk to me. And when she does talk to me, she tells me how much she hates me."

"Fuck, that's rough."

"Yeah."

"Maybe it's time to throw in the towel."

"I still think there's a chance."

"Yeah?" Grave asked. "Are you just too stubborn to admit defeat?"

I looked out the windshield. "Maybe..."

We snuck in through a window in the back of the building. One of our men on the inside made sure to leave it open the night before. Roan was there to attend some kind of charity event, even though it was no secret that he was very uncharitable.

Low-tier drug dealers were stereotypes, with the baggy clothes and the grizzled looks. You could spot one a mile away, but they were only capable of selling an ounce or a tenth. But big-time drug dealers like Roan, they blended into society's aristocrats, hid in plain sight, rubbed elbows with government to get what they wanted.

"You have it?" Grave landed on his feet beside me, in a three-piece gray suit.

I checked my pocket. "Yep."

"Murder by poison. Pretty boring."

"Roan has a lot of allies. It's smart to be anonymous."

"I guess. Still, pussy shit."

We headed down the hallway and into the party. There were at least five hundred people there, all holding their cocktails and talking near standing tables. The crystal chandeliers were made of gold, and an orchestra played Bach.

"Why do they always play classical music?" Grave asked. "It's so fucking cliché."

"You'd prefer Beyoncé?"

"Talk shit about my queen, and I'll shove that poison down your throat."

I rolled my eyes. "Let's focus."

"You know it's hard to focus when I've got Beyoncé on my mind..."

It was easy to blend into the crowd because there were so many people there. No one glanced at us.

"You see him?" I asked.

"No. It's like searching for a needle in a haystack."

"Maybe he's not here yet," I said. "We'll have to wait."

Forty-five minutes later, Roan finally stepped into the building, a blond woman on his arm.

"Talk about being fashionably late..." Grave said.

"You'll cause the distraction. I'll walk by and drop it into his drink. Ready for this?"

Grave surveyed the scene, and his eyes narrowed on a target. "Uh, we've got a problem."

"What?" I followed his eyes until I spotted her.

In a pale-blue dress with a high cut up her thigh, she looked like a princess with the sparkles in the material. Her blond hair had small curls in the strands, and her eyes had blue shadow to match. Her gaze locked on to mine, and as casually as possible, she moved across the room, drawing waves of attention with her.

I nodded to Grave, and we ducked back into the hallway. Otherwise, everyone at the gala would know we were there.

"What's she doing here?" Grave asked.

"Why are you asking me?"

A moment later, Camille rounded the corner, looking like a goddamn supermodel.

I stared at her for a solid twenty seconds, unable to get my head out of the gutter and back in the game.

When Grave realized I was compromised, he took over. "What are you doing?"

"I called Bartholomew." She was careful not to look at me, back to her typical coldness. "He told me about the plan."

"You didn't answer my question," Grave snapped. "What are you doing *here*?"

"I've helped him with this sort of thing before, and I thought I could help you. I'm nobody, so a fake name can get me far. He, or anyone else, sees either of you, game over." She finally looked at me, but the stare was brief before it shifted away again.

"What are you suggesting?" Grave saved. "You deliver the poison?"

"At the very least, I could distract him. I bump into him, get some wine on my chest, and then he'll stare right at my tits for at least five seconds. It's pretty thin material. I take off to the bathroom, and then Cauldron hands the new glass to the waiter and asks him to deliver it. Your faces will never be seen."

Grave seemed to find merit in the plan because he looked at me for approval.

"No."

Camille finally looked at me head on. "Why not—"

"Because this is our problem. Not yours."

"Your well-being is my problem, both of you," she snapped. "Now, let me help."

"You aren't putting yourself at risk—"

"She's just spilling wine on herself," Grave said. "It's not a big deal."

"Not a big deal?" I asked coldly, looking at my brother instead.

"It's definitely less conspicuous than me causing a diversion on the other side of the room. It's less conspicuous than letting anyone see you near him, especially when he drops dead a few hours later. Even if anyone does suspect Camille, no one knows who the hell she is."

Camille shifted her gaze back and forth between us, listening to us argue.

"I don't like this," I said.

"I'll be fine." Camille looked at me with those green eyes, reminding me of a different time, a different reality.

"I think it's a good plan," Grave said. "Now let's do this so we can leave. I have a hot date tonight."

"Does Elise know you're doing this?" Camille asked.

"No," he said sternly. "Like I'd tell her, when she's obsessed with me..."

We all looked at each other for a while before we got moving. Grave stayed behind so he could watch from a distance. I went to the bar, ordered a glass of wine, and then stepped into the hallway to add just enough drops so that the taste would go unnoticed. Mixing it with alcohol would make it more potent, so he would probably collapse much quicker than the typical four hours.

I got into position and waited.

From across the room, Camille gave me a nod in question.

I gave her a nod back to confirm.

Like a pro, she crossed the room and pretended to see someone she knew. She raised her hand, gave a big hello, and so distracted, she ran right into Roan just as he turned around. The glass hit her square in the chest and splashed all over her. The glass toppled out of his hand and onto the floor, where it shattered into pieces. "Oh dear, I'm so sorry." Her hands immediately felt for her chest, soaked in the white wine. As she suspected, the liquid made the material sheer, and without a bra underneath, her tits were easy to see, even from where I stood.

I made my move and asked the waiter to bring him another glass.

He immediately obeyed, like he didn't pay enough attention to know I was a guest and not another waiter. The waiter came over and handed him a new glass, while other staff members came to clean up the mess.

Camille was long gone—and Roan moved with his group to another part of the room to continue their conversation.

It was done.

I dropped off Grave first then headed to Camille's apartment afterward.

She was in the back seat, like I was a taxi driver and she was a passenger. It was a quiet ride home. She still wore my jacket, the front of her chest concealed from view. I pulled up to the curb then killed the engine.

She lingered in the back. "Thanks for the ride."

I looked at her face in the rearview mirror. "Thanks for the help."

"Sure thing." She got out then walked to the front door.

I followed her.

She got the key in the door then turned to me, blocking the entrance. "What are you doing?" And just like that, we were back to where we were before. She loathed me with every fiber of her being, and I groveled in silence.

"So, that's it, huh? We were allies for an hour, and now it's back to pretending I don't exist?"

"Yep." She walked inside and shut the door in my face.

I stood on the threshold, the air cold in my lungs, the concrete having tiny flecks of shiny minerals under the streetlight. I stared at a spot next to my shoe before I turned the handle and welcomed myself inside.

She wasn't in the living room. Must have gone upstairs to take off her wet gown.

I took a seat in the armchair in the living room, one ankle propped on the opposite knee, looking at the fire that had burned out recently. The coals still glowed red, like she'd left the fire unattended to help us.

Minutes later, she came downstairs, dressed in gray sweatpants that were far too big for her and a long-sleeved shirt. She had no bra underneath because I could see her nipples press hard against the material.

She gave a slight jolt when she saw me, like she'd expected me to go in peace.

I stared at her pants for a few seconds. "Those are mine." They were at least ten sizes too big, so long they had to be rolled at the bottom several times so they wouldn't drag on the floor. She must have taken them when she left, a souvenir to remember me by.

"All my stuff is in the wash..." She drew closer, her arms latched across her chest. "I want you to go, Cauldron."

"You do?" I asked. "You were so concerned for my well-being that you involved yourself in this plot, yet you want me to go?"

"Just because I don't want you to die doesn't mean I want to be anywhere near you."

I remained seated.

Her eyes slowly narrowed in annoyance. "Why are you always so stubborn?"

It was impossible to silence the laugh that ripped out of my mouth. "I'm the stubborn one..."

"I asked you to leave, and you won't. That's the definition of the word."

"So what if I'd died tonight? What if Roan had suspected what I was doing and shot me in the stomach? I bled out and died right on the floor?"

She did her best to keep up her angry look, but it was waning.

"I think you'd be pretty upset."

"Like I said a million times, just because I don't want you to die—"

"You still love me."

She went rigid at the accusation, her eyes angry.

"So we're going to make this work."

Her eyebrows slowly furrowed like I'd said the wrong thing. "Love was never the problem, Cauldron. *You* were the problem. That hasn't changed. Sit in that chair all you want. It's not going to change who you are. It's not going to change the fact that you're incapable of not sabotaging every good thing in your life. I've given you plenty of chances, and I won't give you another, not a single one." The fire in her eyes was fueled like gasoline had been splashed right on top. Flames soared into the sky. Her cheeks reddened like she'd been burned. So much anger was stuffed into that small body.

I got to my feet and buttoned the front of my suit.

She immediately stiffened.

I drew close, my eyes homing in on hers.

Out of stubbornness, she wouldn't move.

Fine by me. "I've been a nice guy up until this point. But no more."

Her eyes narrowed. "And what's that supposed to mean?"

I came in closer, our lips almost touching. "I paid for a service. And I expect that service." My eyes switched back and forth between hers, seeing the way she struggled to process that rage.

"Fuck you—"

My hand gripped her by the neck quicker than she could react. Now she was against the wall, winded by my sudden movements, her hands on my wrist and trying to tug free. It was no use. I didn't budge.

Her eyes locked on mine, furious but defeated.

I came in close. So close I could smell champagne on her breath. My eyes watched her lips for a moment before I looked at her once more. She was completely still. Not even breathing. "Be ready at eight."

"Ready for what?"

My fingers squeezed her a little tighter. "Me."

24

CAMILLE

The only option I had was to run.

Pack up my things and disappear.

But that would only buy me time. Cauldron would find me eventually. He'd make good on his word then.

I was screwed—no pun intended.

At eight o'clock, there was no knock on the door.

The asshole just walked in like he owned the place. He stepped into the living room, wearing black jeans and boots with a long-sleeved shirt that fit nicely across his hard chest. The fabric stretched over his arms and shoulders, and it hung loose around his stomach. His hair was slicked back like he'd just taken a shower before heading over here. That meant he would smell like his body soap, a smell I'd tried so hard to forget.

He stared at me with those espresso-colored eyes, just as intense as the day he pointed that gun at me. It was as if we were back in time, full of loathing and lust. "Get your ass upstairs."

"No."

He took a step toward me, his body tight with menace.

"You're going to make me?"

"I'm going to make you do your job."

"What the hell is wrong with you—"

"*You're* the one who walked into that bar and asked for a job. *You're* the one who put yourself at the mercy of men like me. You'd fuck a stranger like Bartholomew, so fuck me instead."

I looked away, so angry because there was no way out of this. This was all my fault. If I'd just taken that job at the art gallery, none of this would be happening. Cauldron wouldn't have found the loophole that put us back into the exact relationship I had fled.

"Now get your ass upstairs." Like a tall statue, he loomed over everything in the room, commanding the place even though the deed was in my name. "Don't make me ask again." He turned away and disappeared up the stairs.

I listened to his footsteps grow fainter as he made it up the stairs and stepped into my bedroom. Then, the house went silent. The floorboards didn't creak. Tension settled on my shoulders because I knew there was no other option. I had to walk up there, swallow my pride and my feelings, and do the job.

I finally mustered the courage to head up the stairs and step into the bedroom.

Cauldron had already made himself comfortable on my bed, sitting up against the pillows at the headboard, buck naked, his dick already hard, probably because he knew I had no other choice than to come up those stairs and do my job.

I tried not to look too hard. It'd been so long since I'd seen him like that, and my typically cold body turned warm. It'd been a long dry spell, and suddenly, those withdrawals hit me when I saw the sexiest man alive waiting for me on my bed. I focused on a spot on his forehead.

"Undress."

I'd been a prostitute for years, but I'd never truly felt like I was doing anything wrong until then. I started with my shirt, pulling it over my head to reveal the lacy bra underneath. My fingers fidgeted at the clasp in the back, taking my time because it was hard to concentrate. I finally got it free and felt the material fall from my arms.

I didn't see his reaction because my focus was below his hairline.

"Eyes."

I sucked in a deep breath before I obeyed. Now, I could see him, see how much he wanted, more than he ever had before.

"Keep going."

I undid my jeans and pulled them down before I stood in the black thong. I kicked away the pants and watched him look me up and down, his big dick against his stomach. My thumbs hooked into my panties, and I slid them down, completing the transition until I was in my bare skin.

I'd never felt so vulnerable. On display. Powerless.

Cauldron enjoyed the sight, his eyes slowly combing over my body like he'd never seen me before. "Get over here."

I didn't move.

His eyes moved to mine again.

"Or I'll come to you."

I gave a twitch of anger before I obeyed. With my heart fluttering in my chest like the wings of a hummingbird, I walked to the side of the bed and approached, seeing his dick get bigger the closer I came. I got onto the bed and straddled his hips—and felt his hard dick right against me.

His hands gripped my hips, and he rocked into me slightly, grinding his hard dick right into my clit.

My hands stayed flattened over my stomach, not touching him at all. But it did feel good, to feel his pressure and his heat.

His arm hooked around my waist and repositioned me onto my back, diagonal across the bed, his heavy weight sinking us both into the cheap mattress. His legs parted my thighs, getting his body into position, bringing us closer together.

I could feel him against me again, hard and hot, anxious.

His face was over mine, looking into my eyes like it was the first time. One hand cupped my face, and he leaned in to kiss me.

I turned away. "No..."

His face rested against my cheek.

"You can fuck me...but not kiss me."

He lay still, his breaths falling against my skin.

I kept my eyes focused on a spot on the wall, my arms forced to my sides so I wouldn't touch the hard stomach I used to graze. My breaths drew in so much air that I sounded like I was running while lying still.

He moved his face down to my neck and kissed me. A single soft kiss. Then another. One at my collarbone. My shoulder. Down my chest to the tops of my tits. A kiss here. A kiss there.

My breathing slowed and my body relaxed. When I closed my eyes, I felt the bumps over my skin. With his scent heavy in my nose, I was taken somewhere else, somewhere in the past, somewhere where my heart was so full it could burst.

He switched sides, kissing the other side of my neck, making his way down again. His arms scooped my legs around his waist, and the maneuver felt so natural that I just went with it. His lips traveled up my neck to my jawline, coming close to my ear, his steady breaths reminding me of whispers shared in the middle of the night. Then he moved down and captured my lips with his, setting my world on fire.

I couldn't interrupt a kiss that demanding. It took control of my lips, took control of my body. His tongue came in soon afterward, dancing with mine like we were back in time. His kiss swept me away, brought a haze over my eyes that blocked out all the heartache. My hands slid up his back and felt the muscles right below the skin. My thighs squeezed his narrow waist. Now that the switch had been flicked on, my body was white-hot, anxious...desperate.

He quickly guided himself inside and sank into my depths.

My nails unleashed and dragged down his back. A thick moan escaped my lips. Pleasure that I'd missed over the past month revitalized my body and made it sing.

He moaned against my lips the second he entered me, a deep, masculine sound, a pleasure that stilled his body for a second before he started to rock into me. His body started to shiver, his breaths turned uneven. He was so deep that he couldn't even kiss me. Just a few seconds after we started, he released with another moan.

Everything came to a standstill. Disappointment hit me hard. I'd burned red-hot a second ago, and now my desire was snuffed out by an unexpected breeze.

But then he started to move inside me again, his dick still the same size as when we began. His lips took mine, and he dominated me once more, grinding me into the sheets, his heavy body rubbing against my clit just right.

My thighs squeezed his body, and my nails dropped like anchors into his skin. I ground back at the same pace, taking the dick I'd longed for all those lonely nights. In the heat of the moment, I forgot how much I hated him. Forgot how much he'd hurt me. It was just toe-curling pleasure.

It approached from a distance, a fireball that was about to set me ablaze. I held on to him harder, lost control of my kiss, feeling it approach with the force of a tidal wave. My eyes dropped down to his powerful chest and the hard muscles of his stomach. My body continued to press into the bed every time he thrust inside me. I was so close, my small body nervous to feel an explosion that big.

"Eyes."

My reaction was automatic. My eyes lifted to his. Intense. Domineering. Affectionate.

He quickened his pace, speeding up his thrusts, grinding into my body harder.

It quickened the arrival and increased the intensity. When it hit me, the tears were automatic. My hips thrust entirely on their own. I was pulled into a moment of euphoria I'd thought I would never feel again. It was a break from reality, from the irreparable damage his betrayal had inflicted.

It passed, and I slowly came back down to earth. His face returned to focus, tinted with red, eyes smoking like a fire burned in his soul. Like a runner at the end of the race, he sprinted to the finish line, thrusting inside me fast and hard, rocking the bed and making the headboard tap against the wall. Then he finished, giving me another load to match the first.

The tight skin over his muscles shone with sweat. He breathed hard as he remained on top of me, his dick slowly softening inside me. With our bodies close together, it was like a summer heat wave. He stayed on top of me like he didn't want to leave.

Once the high was over and reality set in, my mood soured. It was the first time I truly felt like a whore. I felt used. Felt worthless. I was good enough to screw, but I wasn't good enough to love.

I guided him off me then left the bed. With my back turned to him, I quickly pulled on my clothes, knowing his seed was slowly seeping out of me and filling my panties. Then I walked out and headed down the stairs to the living room. I sat on the couch and waited for him to leave.

Moments later, he emerged, fully dressed in the clothes he'd arrived in. He stood there and stared at me, as if he expected me to give an explanation.

I stared at my blank TV, ignoring him.

"That's how it's going to be?" he asked, his voice filled with disappointment.

"You got what you paid for. Now, leave."

"You enjoyed it."

"Maybe I did. But that doesn't mean it meant a damn thing to me."

25

GRAVE

One of her legs was hooked over my shoulder, and she was folded underneath me like a goddamn pretzel. It was one of those nights when once wasn't enough. Not twice either. She had to be sore, but like the consummate professional she was, she never complained.

I could tell when a woman faked an orgasm, and Elise had never faked any of them with me. The tears. The screams. The incoherent moans. It was all real. I paid top dollar to fuck her, but she reaped the same rewards. What I really paid for was passion and affection without commitment. I got to experience all the highs of monogamy without the strings. It was exactly what I needed in my life right now.

With her hands planted on my chest, she came, tears leaking from the corners of her eyes.

I pounded that pussy until I was thoroughly finished, marking my territory and erasing every man who had ever been there. Covered in sweat and catching our breath, we both breathed through the high and the fall. Then I rolled off her and lay on my side of the bed, needing the space to cool off.

Her labored breaths ceased almost immediately. Her eyes were closed, like she was already half asleep. The fire had died down at some point during our fucking, and despite how large the bedroom was, the windows were fogged from our heat.

She turned on her side, makeup running from the moisture she'd shed from her eyes. She seemed knocked out already, fucked into exhaustion.

I stared at the chandelier hanging from the ceiling and slowly cooled off, letting the sweat evaporate from my skin.

My phone vibrated on the nightstand.

The only calls I got this late were work-related, so I reached for the phone and glanced at the name.

There was no name.

I rolled out of bed and moved toward the window to keep quiet. "Grave."

"Sorry to disturb you at this hour, but I thought you should know something." It was a voice I didn't recognize. It belonged to a man who seemed eager to ruin my evening, not apologetic. "I've taken the woman you adore. The only way to get her back is to take her place. If you refuse, I'll fuck her in every hole I can find, and once I'm finally bored with her...which may take a while...I'll kill her. You have twenty-four hours to decide."

I stared at my own reflection in the glass as I listened to all of that. "Who's the woman I adore?"

"Is that how you really want to play this?" he said. "Or should I just kill her now and come for you next?"

"Karl." I didn't recognize the voice, but I recognized the rage. "Roan is playing you. He's the one who switched my patient with your brother—and you're falling right into his trap."

"Maybe. But there's no way to really know, right? Since you killed him and everything..."

I stared at my reflection.

"Twenty-four hours. That's it." Click.

I listened to the dead line for several seconds before I finally lowered the phone to my side. Buck naked, I stood near the glass and stared before I turned around and looked at the woman he should have taken.

She was sitting up in bed, and judging from the horror in her eyes, she'd understood the details of the conversation. "Someone's taken Camille…?"

"I have to call Cauldron. Have my driver take you home." I walked into the closet and pulled on jeans and a long-sleeved shirt before I headed for the door.

Elise was halfway dressed. "Why would someone take her?"

"I told you I have enemies."

"But she has nothing to do with that—"

"That's not how this world works." I left the bedroom and headed to the elevator.

She was right behind me, her shoes in her hand. "Does she know something she could share?"

"No."

"Then what's the point of hurting her?"

"Because it'll hurt me." That was why they took her. I killed Karl's brother. It was only fair to kill the woman I loved.

Elise stood next to me in the elevator, her mouth shut, her eyes averted.

I didn't have the luxury of consoling her. I couldn't alleviate her insecurities. I had twenty-four hours to save Camille's life, and I couldn't spend a single moment on Elise.

I went to Camille's apartment first.

Just on the off chance it was some sick joke. Just on the slim possibility they'd hit the wrong apartment. But one look inside that place confirmed the truth. A lamp was shattered on the floor. The TV was still on even though no one was home. Drops of blood were on the floorboards like someone had been slashed with a knife. There was definitely a struggle.

"Fuck me."

I headed to Cauldron's apartment next. In the middle of the night, I woke up Pius and demanded Cauldron be disturbed. I paced in the sitting room as I waited for him to get his ass out here. My heart was racing with adrenaline, but on the exterior, I looked perfectly calm. I was just as afraid of not getting Camille back as I was of telling my brother what had happened to her.

Cauldron finally made it down the hallway, barefoot and bare-chested, his eyes pissed off because he assumed whatever I needed was trivial and not worth this midnight visit. "What is it?"

There was no good way to say it. None at all. "Karl took Camille."

It took Cauldron a solid five seconds to process it, either because he was still partly asleep or the information was just so terrible he couldn't believe it. "Why would he take Camille?"

"An eye for an eye."

The reality hit him like a punch to the face. His expression changed, the cords in his neck tightening as he clenched his jaw. The veins in his forehead suddenly popped to the surface. His eyes were so angry they deepened in color. It looked like he might let out a scream any second. "What does he want for her?"

"Me."

He stared at me.

"A trade."

After a long stretch of silence, he spoke again. "They'll kill her anyway. They'll just make you watch."

"I know." I'd cut Karl's brother open and put his organs in other people. He wasn't the only one who'd died. The recipients did as well because they weren't a match. It was a fucking catastrophe. So he wanted me to experience the same thing—to watch the person I loved be chopped into pieces. It meant Camille's fate would be horrific. "We'll get her back, alright?"

Cauldron seemed stunned into silence, which was a first.

"Cauldron?"

"How long do we have?"

"Twenty-four hours," I said. "We'll get her back—"

"Damn right, we will. And we'll mutilate every fucker involved. Looks like your business is about to get good..." He walked back down the hallway, probably to get dressed and armed. A handgun or pistol wouldn't do. We'd need some serious shit, like rifles and Uzis.

Minutes later, Cauldron came back packing. A rifle was hanging from one shoulder and a shotgun was across his back. There was an Uzi strapped onto each hip. "Do you know where they are?"

I shook my head.

"We'll trace her phone."

"He'll have destroyed that by now," I said. "When was the last time you saw her?"

"A couple hours ago."

"They must have been watching the place and thought you were me..."

Cauldron closed his eyes briefly, like he was pissed off at himself for not staying. "She threw me out...but I should have stayed."

"You know Camille. It's her way or no way. And remember, if anyone's to blame...it's me."

My brother looked at me again, a mixture of so many hateful emotions, it was hard to tell what he was thinking.

"I was with Elise...but I'm pretty sure that's over now."

"She should be grateful that Karl made the wrong assumption. She'd be the one captured. Her kids would be dead."

"I doubt she's even thought of that." I had more to say, but I kept it to myself because the end of my relationship with Elise was insignificant in the face of our current problem.

"So, what now? We wait for the call?"

"There's got to be somebody we know who might know his whereabouts."

"Karl would have thought of that," Cauldron said. "He would have kept this under wraps from our allies."

With no plan and no one to call, we were packing for no reason. "What about Bartholomew?"

Somehow, Cauldron managed to look even more pissed off.

"He might help us."

"Why? He doesn't owe us anything."

"But he might care for Camille. I bet he could figure out where Karl is with a simple phone call. When Bartholomew calls, people answer."

Cauldron remained silent and angry, just breathing.

"He initially turned down fifty million dollars. That's a lot of money."

He gave a slight nod. "We've got no other leads. Let's do it."

26

CAULDRON

Bartholomew entered the room, a cigar in his mouth and his chest shiny with a hint of sweat. Black sweatpants were low on his hips, and his bare feet hit the hardwood with distinct thuds. He lowered the cigar as a cloud released from the crack between his lips. "Wow. It's the set."

I didn't want to be diplomatic right now. Just cut to the chase and save my girl. But I was the beggar, and beggars couldn't be choosers. When he came close enough, I could recognize the distinct smell of sex.

It was all over him.

He took another puff of the cigar and released the smoke in my face. "What can I do for the Toussaint brothers?"

I didn't correct him. "Camille has been taken."

Bartholomew sat down on the couch, took another puff of the cigar, and then placed it in the ashtray. "By whom?"

I took a seat across from him. Grave did the same. "Karl."

"Are you guessing, or is this confirmed?" He sat back on the couch, arms stretching out on either side.

"He called me," Grave said. "I have twenty-fours to take her place."

Bartholomew shifted his gaze to my brother and studied him for a while. "I heard what you did to his brother. Cold-blooded."

"I didn't know it was him."

"Interesting," he said. "Because I always thought you needed to know everything about a man, down to his blood type, before you put his organs inside someone else."

"Roan switched out the men," Grave said. "He wanted us to be enemies so we would kill each other."

"And even in death, his plan is working." He looked at me next. "You just got your girl back, and this happens... What a shame."

"Help us," I blurted, unable to word it in a tactful way.

"Me?" Bartholomew asked. "I was nice enough to sell her to you. I've always been a hopeless romantic…"

"One phone call and you could figure out where he is," I said. "Where he's holding her."

He propped the side of his head on his closed knuckles and stared at me. "Our mission with Roan was a success. No one suspects I had anything to do with it, even though I'm the one who gains the most. I'd be stupid to roll the dice again so soon."

"If we don't get her back, you know what will happen to her." I leaned forward in the chair, locking my eyes on this man in desperation.

He held my gaze for a long time before he, too, sat forward, arms on his knees. "And you know what will happen the second Grave hands himself over. You'll lose your woman *and* your brother."

"That's why I need the upper hand," I said, trying to keep my voice steady, even though I wanted to scream. "Get this information for me. We'll storm in there and kill every one of those motherfuckers."

Bartholomew rubbed his hands together, lost in thought.

"You must care for her," I said. "You didn't want to sell her."

"Because she was useful to me. A lot of my men are useful to me. Doesn't mean I care about them."

Grave took over. "Camille is an innocent person. She's not part of this world."

"She became part of this world the second she sold herself for money," Bartholomew said. "And she knows that. What I don't understand is...why did they take Camille for Grave?" His eyes flicked to me. "You look alike, but not that much alike."

"It's complicated," I said, not wanting to dive into ancient history right now.

Bartholomew grinned, like he'd figured it out. "Now I wish I'd taken a hit when I had the chance. She must be something else."

In any other moment, I would pick up that hot cigar and shove it in his eyes. But I kept still and swallowed the rage. "Help us, Bartholomew. We have no leads, and if we don't get to her before the twenty-four-hour deadline, she'll be gone."

"What's in it for me?" he asked.

"Name your price," I said. "Between the two of us, we can make it happen."

"You should know me by now," Bartholomew said. "Money isn't an effective motivator. I move millions every single day. Every single hour, probably."

"Then what do you want?" I asked.

He looked slightly amused. "Camille."

My heart dropped like a rock. "What the fuck did you say?"

"You heard me, Cauldron. I want Camille back."

Grave looked at me, staying quiet because there was nothing he could add to the conversation.

Would this nightmare ever fucking end? "You even said yourself she didn't want to be with you."

"That's not why I want her. She was a good wingman. No one ever expects a woman to be a criminal. And the prettier she is, the more innocent she seems. I want her back on the job, at my beck and call. Ball's in your court."

I sucked in a long breath to dull my nerves, but they were on fire.

"We both know she enjoyed the work," he said. "I'll even pay her if she wants."

I didn't want her in the criminal limelight. I didn't want her exposed. I just wanted to take her back home and disappear from this god-awful world. "Fine...we have a deal."

27

CAMILLE

My arms were so close to my body I couldn't move at all. A thick rope had been secured around my shoulders, torso, and waist, keeping my arms so tight against my body my shoulders were about to pop out of the sockets. It was payback for the way I'd cut one of his guys when they came to the house. I knocked the other one out cold with a lamp. But it still wasn't enough for me to get away.

Now I was stuck in the parlor of an apartment in the city, men standing guard behind where I sat on the couch. The one in charge came in and out, smoking a cigar or drinking booze. I had no idea why I was there, but I suspected it had something to do with Cauldron or Grave.

Maybe both.

The man in charge was audible in the other room. A couple guys called him Karl, so I had a name for the face. His voice was quiet because of all the obstacles in the way, but I could make out what he said. "When Grave shows up, we don't make the exchange. We're going to tie him up and force him to watch us cut that bitch open and take out each organ until she flatlines. Her death will be the same as my brother's."

My entire body went cold when I heard what he said.

Cut me open.

Take me apart—piece by piece.

Holy fucking shit.

I was on the verge of a panic attack when I remembered what Grave and Cauldron were both capable of. They were two powerful men who would get me back. They would... I knew they would. I just had to stay calm.

Karl took a call. I could tell by the way his tone changed. "Bartholomew. To what do I owe the pleasure?"

I gave a gasp so loud that one of the men guarding me came around the couch and looked at me straight on. With one eyebrow cocked, he examined me with suspicion.

I improvised as best I could. "These ropes are so tight... I can't breathe." I made the same gasp again to add credibility to my lie. "Could you loosen them just a bit? Please."

He gave me a cold look before he returned to his position behind me.

Karl talked about business, something about a dead drop...whatever that was. But then the conversation changed. "I'm kinda busy right now, Bartholomew. Let's meet tomorrow."

My heart was racing.

"I don't understand why this can't wait until tomorrow."

This was no coincidence.

"Alright," Karl said. "Make it quick. Here's the address..."

I knew they were coming. Cauldron, Grave, and Bartholomew. They were coming. Now I just had to sit there and wait...

A couple hours later, I heard Bartholomew's voice. "Nice place, old man."

Karl chuckled at the backhanded insult. "Old man? I could take you in a knife fight."

"Just tell me when and where."

Very weird banter...

"Before we discuss business, I need a drink." Bartholomew's footsteps came close to the hallway.

I did my best to act normal in front of the guards, but my breathing had picked up quite a bit.

"Ignore the woman in there," Karl said after him.

"I will—as long as she's not naked." His footsteps grew louder and louder. Then he appeared, in his black leather jacket, his military-style boots, with his dark hair slicked back. He walked in like he owned the place and headed straight to the bar without looking at me.

It took all my strength not to scream.

He moved behind the bar and grabbed the bottle and the glass. As he poured the drink, he lifted his gaze and looked at me.

"Help me," I mouthed.

Bartholomew looked down again, as if he hadn't noticed. "Got any cigars?"

Neither of the men moved.

Bartholomew looked up again. "I'm talking to you two idiots."

One of them walked away, moving into another room.

I knew Bartholomew was up to something. I'd seen him in action, seen the way he made things happen in the most subtle ways.

"Where do you keep the good stuff?" Bartholomew took a drink then poured it down the drain. "Donkey piss, that's what this is." He kneeled down behind the bar.

The other guard moved and joined him, unlocking one of the cabinets.

Bartholomew slammed his head onto the corner of the cabinet. It was a quiet thud, and then it was silent.

I gave a quiet gasp, a gasp no one seemed to hear.

Bartholomew quietly lowered the guard's body to the floor, hidden behind the bar. Then he moved across the room to where the second guard had disappeared. I didn't hear anything, and when Bartholomew returned, he returned alone. He pulled out a knife and sliced through the ropes.

"Thank—"

He held his finger to his lips, his eyes furious.

I felt the ropes go loose. I could finally take a full breath.

He pulled out a gun from the back of his jeans and handed it to me. In a whisper so quiet I barely heard him, he said, "Hide. Shit's about to go down."

I took the cold gun in my hands and gave a nod.

"You have two minutes." He grabbed his drink and headed back to the room, and as if nothing had happened, he continued their conversation. "Did you hear about Roan? I'm not sure what I'm going to do now that distribution has been halted..."

I got free of the rope and crept to a different part of the apartment. I opened the first door I came across and saw that it was an empty guest room. I snuck inside and shut the door before I entered the closet. I shut that door, got comfortable on the floor, and waited.

The sound of gunfire exploded.

It was utterly silent one moment, and then it was hell the next. I was cocooned by two doors, but I still covered my ears and lay flat on the floor. I worried these walls wouldn't be enough to stop the bullets that might hit me by mistake.

The gunfire continued. There would be moments of silence in between the noise, but then the shots would fire again. It seemed to stretch for an eternity, but in reality, it was probably less than two minutes.

Then it was quiet. And it stayed quiet.

I wanted to burst out of the closet and run for Cauldron, but I knew better than to blindly reveal myself.

Then I heard his voice. "Camille! It's safe!"

I continued to lie at the bottom of the closet, breathing through the relief. For a moment, I'd thought I was going to end up on a gurney, paralyzed by drugs so my organs could be harvested. But Cauldron had come for me...and so did Grave.

"Camille!" Now it was Grave. "Come out!"

I left the closet and the bedroom and stepped into the hallway. When I rounded the corner, I found Cauldron in the room where I'd been tied up, the ropes at his feet. I saw him before he saw me, saw the anguish on his face even though all our enemies were dead. The cords in his neck were so tight they were about to snap. Then he turned my way, and when his eyes settled on me, he looked paralyzed. "Baby."

I rushed to him, sprinting into his arms.

He caught me and squeezed me hard against his chest. His grip was so tight it seemed like he would never let me go. Not in a million years. His forehead rested on my head, and he cupped the back of my neck, his chest pushing against my face with every deep breath he took. He dropped his lips and kissed me on the forehead. "I'm so sorry."

"It's not your fault, Cauldron."

He pulled away, his eyes focused on mine. "I'm sorry that I fucked this up..."

We stood outside the bar, the cold night air like death's fingers through my hair. Winter had been brutal this year, freezing cold and full of heartbreak. I approached Bartholomew, leaving the guys behind so we could speak in private. "Thank you for everything. Cauldron tells me you're the only reason they were able to find me."

With his hands in the pockets of his jeans and his limber body leaning against the lamppost, he looked at me with that subtle smile on his lips. "Don't thank me just yet. I only stuck out my neck for something in return."

"Which is?"

"You." He leaned forward slightly, pointing at me with his body. Then he leaned back. "Me. Back to our former arrangement."

"As in...Cauldron's contract is over?"

"No. More of an à la carte situation. When I need a wingman, I'll call you. Based on what Cauldron's told me, it sounds like you've missed me. The feeling is mutual because not every woman can pull off this sort of thing."

I should be thrilled, but I was somewhat disappointed.

He picked up on it. "I was under the impression you enjoyed the work."

"I enjoyed having duties outside of my usual work."

"I'd pay you for your time. Consider it a side hustle."

"Do I have a choice?" I asked.

He stared at me long and hard.

"I guess that's a no..."

"I'm not a fan of coercion. You should know that by now. But I think it's a small favor to ask in exchange for everything I risked to get you out of there. This is the moment where you decide who you want to be. Are you loyal to your allies? Or are you out for only yourself?"

"That's what we are?" I asked. "Allies? Friends?"

"Whoa. Wouldn't take it that far."

"Are Cauldron and Grave friends?"

"God, no."

"Then what constitutes a friend?"

He gave a shrug. "Honestly, I don't know—as I have none."

Cauldron drove me home, but when he turned the wrong direction, I realized he had different plans.

"Where are you going?"

"Home."

"Well, *my* home is the other way."

"Come on, baby. I'm not letting you stay alone tonight."

I still winced when I heard the endearment. It didn't fit anymore, like a shirt that was too tight. "Karl and all his men are dead. Roan's gone. What's there to be afraid of, exactly?"

"You must be shaken up—"

"They just tied me up and put me in a chair. That was it."

He kept driving. "I know you're brave—"

"It's not like they pointed a gun at me and pulled the trigger..."

Cauldron gave a quiet sigh. "Is this really how we're going to do things?"

"I just want to go home, Cauldron."

"Well, I've paid for your time, and I want you at my place."

"Gonna pull that card, huh?"

"You're giving me no choice."

We sat in silence for the rest of the drive, the city quiet because it was an hour before sunrise. It was so cold there was frost across the gardens in front of the apartments. A few minutes later, we arrived at his apartment, sealed with warmth the second we were in the elevator. The parlor was dark, like his servants hadn't been disturbed when he left hours ago.

Cauldron took his jacket and hung it on the coatrack.

I purposely avoided his look. "I'll sleep in the guest room—"

"You'll sleep with me."

"I'm not screwing you—"

"Not asking you to." He faced me, squaring his shoulders like I was an opponent. "So let me get this straight. You're taken as a hostage, and the second you're free, you run straight into my arms, but I mean nothing to you? We make love, but then it's like it never happened? How can you hate me *this* much? How can you hate me when I've told you how goddamn sorry I am?"

My arms crossed over my chest, and I looked away.

"I'm actually asking you."

"How?" My head snapped back in his direction. "Because none of it means anything when I say I love you and you don't say it—"

"I love you."

The breath I sucked between my teeth was involuntary. It was like a hiss, like he hit me in the face rather than spoke a beautiful confession.

His eyes remained steady, full of sincerity, bright like the Eiffel Tower. "I'm sorry that it took this long for me to admit it. Not just to you. But to myself."

I was stunned into silence because that was the last thing I expected from him.

"I'm sorry that it took the threat of losing you to force it out of me."

I still didn't know what to say.

"Please forgive me."

I looked away.

"Give me another chance."

"I'm scared..." My eyes remained focused on a painting on the wall.

"And you have every right to be."

"I can't just go back to our relationship like nothing happened."

"I'm not asking you to. I'm asking for another chance. That's all."

"You say it like it's so simple…" When I looked at him again, I felt the tears in my eyes, felt their weight as they shifted to my eyelids and bulged into drops. "You say it like this relationship hasn't been an uphill battle from day one. In my armor, I fought for you every single day, and you never did a damn thing. You never even wanted me in the first place—"

"But I want you now. More than anything. More than anyone." His voice turned desperate, fighting for me with everything he had. "I know this is an asshole thing to say, but you're never going to love anyone the way you love me. I'm not going to love another woman ever. You didn't sleep with Bartholomew because you're as committed to me as you ever were."

My eyes moved to him.

"He told me."

Bastard.

"I'm sorry, but I see your hand. I see your cards. Making this work with me is the only hand you have to play."

"No, it's not—"

"Not if you want to be happy."

I looked away again, tears dripping down my cheeks.

He kept his distance. "Be happy with me."

"Be happy until you change your mind? Be happy until you throw me out of the house? Be happy until—"

"I'll do the husband thing. I'll do the father thing. I'll walk away from the business. I'll do anything to bring you home."

With my body planted in the opposite direction, I imagined the life he'd just described. A small ceremony with just us and his father and brother. Small diamonds woven into my white gown. All my things in his bedroom. Going to sleep with him beside me. Waking up and enjoying breakfast together on the terrace. Then one little person...and then another little person. A family of four. A family of my own. "Do you want those things?"

"No. But I do with you."

"Don't tell me things I want to hear just to—"

"I'm not. Come live with me, and that's the life we can have. Not tomorrow. But someday."

My arms were locked so tight they actually hurt my ribs. It was tempting to go back, especially when the reward was a dream come true. "Why did all these terrible things have to happen for you to give me what I wanted?"

"Because I'm an idiot."

"I still don't think you understand how much you hurt me. I don't think you ever will."

"Not true."

I turned around to look at him through watery eyes.

"If you don't give me another chance...I'll understand exactly."

28

ELISE

Can we talk?

I'd been waiting on pins and needles for Grave to reach out. *You're okay?*

I'm fine, sweetheart.

I was worried.

I'm always fine, so never worry.

I can come to you.

See you then.

I'd kept my nanny around because I knew I would need her at the drop of a hat. I changed my clothes and drove to Grave's apartment. After a long ride in the elevator, I finally entered the warmth of his apartment.

It was almost ten in the evening, so I wasn't greeted with a spread and champagne from Raymond.

Grave came down the hallway, looking sexy as hell in just his sweatpants. Muscular and strong, with a sharp jawline that cast a shadow down his neck, he looked like he belonged on a calendar instead of in the streets. He walked over to me, slid his big hands around my waist then down to my ass as he pulled me in for a kiss.

Like a piece of chocolate in your mouth, I melted. I always melted for this man.

When he tried to pull away, I latched on to him, not wanting the embrace to end.

His arms returned to their former tightness, and he rested his chin on my forehead. His scent was a mixture of masculinity and pine, like he'd just chopped wood in the snow.

"Is Camille alright?"

Once her name was mentioned, there was a long beat, like he didn't want to talk about her. "We got her back. She's fine."

"Good."

He pulled away, moving far enough back that he could see my face. "She's staying with Cauldron. I imagine this will bring them back together."

"Yeah...hopefully."

A long stretch of silence ensued, the two of us looking at each other, thinking the same thing but not acknowledging it.

Grave spoke first. "When Cauldron left Camille's apartment, they thought it was me."

Here we go. "But they were watching her apartment because they knew what she meant to you."

"Yes. *Meant.*" He was soft with me a moment before, but now he hardened, turning to impenetrable stone. "We've had this conversation before. I'm in no mood to have it again. I'm grateful for their idiocy because I'd much rather them take her than you. Or worse—your children."

It was such a horrible thought that I couldn't even bring myself to think it.

"Let this go, Elise."

"You know me so well..."

"You can't be this intimate with someone without knowing all their tells. You're the woman in my life, and I want to keep it that way. I'm happy. Happier than I've been in a long time."

"It's not really about her..."

He let out an irritated sigh.

"It's about you."

"Do I compare myself to your ex-husband? Do you think I feel insecure that you loved someone enough to marry them? I don't."

"Wow, you really have no idea." He couldn't return my feelings because he didn't even know what they were. This man was brilliant, but he was also oblivious. "Looks like you don't know all my tells after all."

His gaze hardened before he looked away.

"I'm in love with you."

His eyes remained averted before they slowly made their way back to me.

For just a tiny moment, I prayed he would say it back, hoped it would be written in his eyes.

But he said nothing.

"I think you already knew that...even though you pretended otherwise."

"I don't want this to end, so no, I didn't acknowledge it."

He should have just punched me in the face. It would have hurt a lot less. "Wow...okay."

"Don't act like I'm the asshole here."

"Then what are you?" I snapped, hiding the hurt in my voice by sounding angry instead.

He stepped closer to me, his eyes furious. "The first night we met, you laid down the law. You said it was a meaningless relationship, and if I ever tried to make it more, we'd be done. Now you're breaking your own rules, rules that I agreed to. I'm the asshole? You came to me under false pretenses."

"Things change—"

"That's bullshit. Your kids will be in the house for more than a decade. That hasn't changed."

"I'd be willing to bring you into our lives—"

"No."

He could have stabbed me, and that'd still hurt less. "You wanted to marry Camille and have a family..."

"That's different."

"Different because you love her and not me?" How could we be so close and he feel nothing? How could we have the most passionate relationship of my life and it was unremarkable to him?

He looked away, refusing to answer the question.

"So you are still in love with her."

"No."

"Then how is it different?"

"Because I want my own kids." He looked at me again, his face tinted with red. "I don't want to be a stepfather. There, I fucking said it."

That hurt most of all.

Grave turned away, his arms shaking he was so mad. "This was supposed to be a meaningless relationship, but you pulled the fucking bait-and-switch trick on me. I thought I was getting a no-strings-attached fuck-a-thon with a woman who couldn't want something more, and you fucked me over. You think I want to say these things to you?"

I was on the verge of tears, tears I couldn't contain. I told this man I loved him, and he stripped me down to nothing. When my kids opened their presents under the Christmas tree, I'd pictured Grave there with us, bonding with my son, being protective of my daughter, dreaming of a life where I could have everyone I loved under the same roof. I imagined him as my husband, fucking me first thing in the morning before he left for work and again before we went to sleep. It was a dream come true.

But now that I knew how he really felt, it wasn't a dream...but a fucking fantasy.

Tears pouring down my face, sobs about to crack my chest, I made it back to the elevator and hit the button so hard it slightly turned in the socket. But it still lit up like it was functioning. I threw my coat over my shoulders, and thankfully, the doors opened immediately.

I hit the button and faced the back of the elevator, not wanting him to see me ugly cry. Not wanting him to know that he'd hurt me far more than my ex-husband ever did. The doors shut, and I finally started to move downstairs.

He didn't come after me.

This was it—the end.

29

GRAVE

"Sir, Camille is here to see you." My butler Raymond entered my study with his hands behind his back, glasses on the bridge of his nose.

I sat behind my desk, my eyes tired because I'd been up all night. I got some work done, but all of it was half-assed. "Send her away."

He gave a slight bow then disappeared.

I sank in my chair and looked out the window. It was raining. Raindrops pelted the window frame like tiny little drums.

He returned moments later. "Sir, she insists."

"Well, I insist on her getting the fuck out of my house." My voice rose immediately, going from zero to sixty in a fraction of a second.

Even my butler gave a flinch at my anger.

Camille appeared behind him, following the voices like a trail of breadcrumbs.

My butler looked at her then looked at me.

I gave her a furious stare before I looked out the window again.

My butler left the room, closing the door behind him.

Camille stared at me for a few seconds before she sat in one of the chairs facing my desk.

"I don't want to talk about it."

"Talk about what?"

My face slowly turned back to hers, seeing the genuine surprise on her face.

"What's wrong?" she asked. "Why are you so angry?"

Maybe she didn't know. "I just said I didn't want to talk about it, didn't I? What do you want?"

She watched me for a few seconds, her eyes shifting back and forth between mine. "Did something happen with—"

"Goddammit." I slammed my fist down hard, and she jumped. "What do you want?"

Now she was quiet. She just examined me from across the desk. Her breaths were quicker, like my sudden outburst still made her uneasy. It'd been a long time since she'd seen me like this. Probably brought back a lot of memories. "Um...I don't know what to do about Cauldron. But you seem to be having a rough day, so I'll just go..."

"Why are you asking me?"

"Because I know you'll tell me the truth. You can be impartial since you know us separately."

"What did he say to you?"

"He'll marry me and have kids with me. Wants me to give him another chance..." She looked out the window for a while. "Told me he loved me...first time I've ever heard him say that."

I studied her face, seeing all the uneasiness around her mouth. "Isn't that what you wanted?"

"I'm just afraid that a couple months down the road, he'll change his mind." She fidgeted with her hands. "I can't get my heart broken again. I've done it so many times... I don't think I'd survive it."

"You don't owe him anything, Camille. If the answer is no, the answer is no."

"I want the answer to be yes," she said. "I want all those things. Do you think...he means it?" She looked to me for guidance. Sometimes it was hard to believe that our relationship had transformed into this. A friendship.

"I've never heard Cauldron say those things to a woman, so I assume it's how he really feels."

"So you think I should give our relationship another chance?"

"I didn't say that."

"Well, now I'm asking you."

Fuck, that was a loaded question. "I don't believe my brother would say those things if he didn't mean them. He has faults, but lying isn't one of them. You should have seen him when I told him you'd been taken. He didn't scream or cry, but he had this look on his face...a look I'd never seen before. It was raw anguish."

Her eyes dropped.

"When you guys were separated, he looked miserable. He sat on my couch and passed out from all the booze he drank. To put that into perspective, my brother drinks all the time, so his tolerance is insane. For him to be knocked out like that, he probably had alcohol poisoning. I think my brother's love for you is real, and he's been struggling with those feelings this entire time, since the beginning. When he told you he loved you, that wasn't the first time he realized it. He's known for a long time but refused to say it."

"Last time I talked to you, you said he wouldn't change."

"And that was before he changed. That was before he grew some balls and said this shit to you."

"So...it sounds like I should give him another chance?"

I gave a shrug. "It's your decision, Camille. Only you know what's right."

"He told me I didn't have a choice...because I'll never love anyone the way I love him."

"Based on what I've seen, that's probably true."

She gave a slight nod.

"Go for it, Camille. If he fucks up again, then you can move on without looking back."

"God...that would kill me."

"I think walking away without trying would kill you more."

Her gaze dropped, like that alternate reality flashed before her eyes in mere seconds. She remained silent, lost in thought, deep in contemplation. It was like I wasn't there anymore. "Thank you for talking with me."

"Yeah." We'd never talked this much when we were together. She never opened up to me the way she did now, even when we were sleeping together. I guess being paid always made her withdrawn, always made her treat it as a job rather than a life. Elise had never been like that with me. That shit felt real.

She looked at me once again, and I knew what was coming. "What do you not want to talk about?"

Now I was the one who looked away.

"You assumed I already knew...but it's not Cauldron. Must be Elise."

"Aren't you smart?"

"What happened?" Despite the savageness in my voice, she always kept her tone gentle.

"We're over."

"Why?"

"Because we are." My eyes remained on the window, watching new raindrops form on the glass then streak down like rivers.

"You can talk to me."

My eyes shifted back to her. "You're the woman I wanted to marry. I thought you would give me strong sons and beautiful daughters. No, I can't talk to you. Not about this." I looked away again.

It was quiet. Like the conversation was over. She just needed to get up and leave. "Neither one of us feels the way we used to. I used to hate you...and now I love you."

I fought against the urge as hard as possible, but my desperation won. My head turned so I could look at her face. It was the first time she'd said that to me, and probably the only time she would say it.

"And I know your feelings for me have evolved. Now you care for me like a sister. Care for me like your friend."

"I don't have any friends."

"You're wrong about that because you have at least one—me."

My eyes shifted away.

"What happened with Elise?"

"She ruined it. That's what."

"And how did she do that? Because I know she's far too hung up on you to sleep around or betray your trust."

I gave a slight smile because she was closer than she realized. "She told me she loved me."

Camille was quiet.

I looked at her again, wanting to see her reaction.

"Dumping her was an asshole response."

"And I'm an asshole, so there you go."

"No, you aren't. Why would you do that to her?"

I tried to keep my anger in check, but it was impossible. "Because she made a big speech about her rules. You know what her rules are? To never want anything more, because the second I ask for more, she'll dump me. She was very clear about that. She lured me into a false sense of security, made me think I could be present in that relationship because there was no future, but that was all a bunch of bullshit."

"That's not what happened—"

"And you would know? I'm sorry, were you there?"

Camille gave me that hard gaze, the one that warned impending doom. "She's never had a client who meant anything to her, so it's never been an issue. And then she met you…and she got swept off her feet. She's human, Grave."

I looked away again.

"I know you care about her."

"Of course I do."

"And I know the reason you're so angry right now is because you didn't want to lose her."

My jaw went tight because she'd hit the nail right on the head.

"You weren't ready for it to end."

I ignored her.

"So, get her back."

"I can't." My head turned back to her. "The second she put that out in the open, everything changed. I can't just go back to what we were because it doesn't exist anymore. I was just a man with a whore, but now…"

"You're a man with a woman."

I listened to the raindrops pelt against the window. "That's not what I wanted—"

"But it's what happened. And I know you'll never admit it, not even to yourself, but I know you love her too."

My eyes darted back to her so fast. "Don't tell me how I feel—"

"I'm not telling you anything. I'm acknowledging it."

"This isn't the relationship that I wanted. Period. When I hired her, I just wanted something easy, something to forget...the past." Now I wouldn't look at her. "The last thing I want is another relationship."

"Well, you're in one, whether you like it or not."

"I'm not ready for marriage—"

"Did she ask to get married?" Camille asked skeptically. "Grave, all she did was tell you how she feels."

"How does that nursery rhyme go? First comes love, then comes marriage...then the baby in the baby carriage? The second she said that, she terminated the best thing that had ever happened to me."

"Grave—"

"I don't want to be a stepfather. I told her that."

Camille's eyes fell, like she knew how much that must have hurt Elise.

"I felt like shit for saying it, but she needs to understand..."

"Have you met her kids?"

I clenched my jaw before I answered. "No."

"Then how do you know that's something you don't want?"

"Would you want to raise kids that Cauldron had with some other woman?" I asked incredulously.

"His kids would be my kids," she said gently. "So, yes."

She was a woman, so I shouldn't have asked her.

"You can still have your own kids, Grave. I'm sure she would want to have your babies."

I focused on the window.

"You shouldn't throw this away. You should at least give it a chance."

"I already told you I'm not ready for this—"

"You aren't ready to love a woman you already love?" she asked, bewildered. "You say you aren't ready for it, but you're already living it. You just refuse to acknowledge it...which is pretty cowardly."

My head snapped back in her direction. "Watch it, Camille."

"Look, you'll hate yourself if you don't at least try. Because Elise is going to get a new client, and that'll eat you alive. And then one day, she'll find someone who loves her kids as their own...and you'll be alone."

30

CAULDRON

It'd been raining the last few days. I spent my time sitting in front of the fire in my study. Sometimes I lay in bed long after my alarm went off. I skipped the gym —which was unheard of. But I just didn't have it in me.

I wound up on her doorstep, the rain soaking my coat as I stood there. Water dripped to the edge of my nose before it splattered on the ground. I rang the doorbell and waited, feeling like I was taking a cold shower.

She opened the door and narrowed her eyes in concern. "It's pouring out there. Where's your umbrella?"

Men like me didn't own umbrellas.

She pulled me inside. "You're soaking wet."

I stripped off my jacket and then kicked off my shoes.

"Let me put these in the dryer for you." She carried everything to another room.

My pants were still soaking wet, and I couldn't sit on anything without causing a puddle, so I stripped them off. Took off the shirt too.

Camille came back into the room and did a double take. "Um...I'll put these in the dryer too." She gathered my things and walked away.

I took a seat on the couch in my black boxers, leaving my phone and wallet on the coffee table.

When she returned, she draped a blanket over my shoulders.

It was the first time she'd shown me affection, so I didn't stop her.

"What are you doing here?" She tightened the blanket around me before she sat on the edge of the coffee table and faced me.

"You won't return my calls or texts." She'd given me her answer without actually giving it, and it was like a bullet lodged in a rib. It hurt every time I tried to breathe. I'd come this far and fought this hard, only to lose at the very end.

She dropped her chin and deflected the statement.

She was the only reason I was still in Paris. Didn't care for the city as much as Grave did. Preferred my own space. Preferred my own land. But Camille was home now, so wherever she was, so was I.

"I'm still thinking it over…"

It'd been days since we'd last spoken. Days of isolation and loneliness.

"Is that okay?"

It was utterly disappointing. "As long as your answer isn't no, I'm happy."

She crossed her legs and brought her hands together. The rain started to fall harder now, like a stampede of hooves on the roof. She looked up at the ceiling before she looked at me again. "How long are you in Paris?"

"Until you're ready to come home with me."

She stared at me, subtle emotion in her eyes. "I don't know what to do…"

I closed my eyes as the pain flooded everywhere.

"I asked Grave for his advice."

"And what did my brother say?" He didn't always have the highest opinion of me. Said straight to my face that I'd never change. If he still had feelings for Camille, it would be the perfect opportunity to put a nail in my coffin and get rid of me forever.

"That it'll kill me not to try..."

Thank you, Grave. "Then try."

"It's not so simple. I'm not sure when our relationship was ever real. It started on a lie. And then I asked for more, and you were very cold about that. I'm not even sure—"

"It was real the moment I told you I loved you. That's where we begin."

Her eyes bored into mine.

"We can take things as slow as you want. I don't care about the specifics, just as long as we're together."

"Then maybe we shouldn't live together..."

It was a disappointment because I wanted her in my bed every night. It was ironic since I'd tried so hard to keep her away for so long. "If that's what you want. I can do my business from Paris, so you can continue to live here."

She gave a nod. "Okay."

I finally got a yes. I finally got something good out of her. "Can I take you to dinner tomorrow night?"

"Sure. But I was just about to make dinner...if you'd like to join me."

It was the first time I felt good. Felt like everything would be okay. "I'd love to."

We lay on the couch together, watching TV. She was wrapped in my arms, leaning against my chest with her head just under mine. The fire had gone out a while ago, and I could tell she was asleep based on the way her breathing had changed. The show ended and something else came on, but I didn't dare move, not when she was in my arms like this. We'd never done this before. Never snuggled together on a couch or in a bed as we watched TV.

It was nice.

She stirred thirty minutes later, taking a deep breath when she came to. She turned her neck to look up at me, her eyes tired like she wanted to keep sleeping. "Sorry..."

"It's alright." I pressed a kiss to her temple.

She turned to face me, her little body still wrapped in my arms. "You're comfortable."

"Yeah?"

"And warm."

"Good thing, since the fire went out."

With sleepy eyes, she looked at me, looked at me like she didn't want to stop. "I'd invite you to sleep over, but..."

"But what?"

"You know..."

My eyes flicked back and forth between hers. "I'm fine just sleeping with you, baby."

"Yeah?"

"I'd much rather sleep here with you than alone in my apartment...missing you."

After a half smile, we locked up the house and went upstairs to her bedroom. She washed her face in the bathroom before she joined me under the covers, snuggling into my body just the way she had on the couch.

We were locked together, her leg over my hip, the two of us sharing a single pillow. She was just in a t-shirt and her panties, and it was hard to keep myself limp so I wouldn't jab her all night long.

"Have you talked to Grave?" she asked out of nowhere.

"No. Why?"

"He broke up with Elise."

"Why?"

"She said she loved him."

"Oh."

"I tried to talk some sense into him, but it didn't work. Maybe you'll have better luck."

"He listens to you more than he listens to me."

"I think he values your opinion a lot more than you realize..."

Grave was already at the bar when I arrived.

He seemed to be on his second or third drink.

"Bad day?" I sat on the stool beside him.

"You could say that."

I tapped my fingers on the surface and ordered a round. "What happened?"

"Good old-fashioned bullshit."

"I heard about Elise."

When he got another glass, he downed it quickly. "Guess that means you're spending time with Camille."

"I slept over the other night."

"Good for you."

"It's not that good. She wants to take it slow."

He turned to look at me. "You should be grateful she wants to take anything at all with you."

"Trust me, I am. And I know what you're doing."

His stare deepened.

"Deflecting me from Elise."

He hit his glass on the table. "You want to talk about it? Fine. Let's talk about it."

"For starters, you look like shit."

"Your face is about to look like shit if you keep it up."

"You look miserable."

"That's just how my face looks."

"No, it's not. It doesn't have to be this way."

He finished his glass then ordered another. "I'm guessing Camille gave you the rundown."

"Yeah."

"You told me yourself you were jealous that I had a relationship with a woman who vehemently didn't want anything more. No strings. No commitment. No bullshit. Well, she pulled the bait-and-switch on me..."

"It sounds like she fell in love."

"She told me that would never happen."

"I didn't think I'd fall for my brother's lover, but here we are."

He looked at me, his eyes cold and guarded.

"You're being hypocritical, you know that?"

"How?"

"You broke the rules too. She just has the balls to admit it."

He slid his glass closer to him. "I'm this close to smashing this over your head."

"Wouldn't be the first time."

Instead of cracking my skull, he chose to take a drink.

"Have you learned nothing from my mistakes?"

"She has kids, Cauldron. Don't pretend nothing would be different with Camille if she had children."

"Yeah, it would be different. But I think I would at least try."

He stared into his glass. "I'm done talking about this."

I let the matter drop. "Just don't drag your feet too long..."

"My boys." Our father entered the bar, gripping each one of us by the shoulder. "The three of us together... a dream come true." He patted the backs of our heads before he moved to the hostess stand. "Let's eat."

Grave was quiet throughout dinner. Didn't seem like he was even paying attention to anything Father said. His mind probably on Elise or thinking about everything I'd said. The only man I'd met more stubborn than myself was Grave. The guy could be a goddamn mule.

"Everything alright?" Father asked when he noticed.

Grave slowly returned to the conversation. "I've got a lot on my mind."

"Isn't that always the case?" Father asked.

"Now it's more than usual." He left his chair and buttoned the front of his jacket. "Excuse me." He crossed the restaurant and headed to the restrooms.

Father turned his gaze on me. "Your brother seems worse, but you seem better. Quite the switch."

After hitting rock bottom, I found it made me eerily calm. "He's going through a hard time."

"Anything I should be worried about?"

"Just a woman."

"Ah, I see." He drummed his fingers lightly on the table. "How are things with Camille?"

"Rocky. But improving."

"She wants a ring, and you won't give it to her," he said before he took a drink of his wine.

"The opposite. I fucked up, and she's struggling to forgive me."

"Don't worry, she will."

I questioned him with my gaze.

"She's not stupid. She knows how lucky she'd be to land a guy like you. A Toussaint."

"Beaufort," I corrected.

"I respect your allegiance to your mother, but she'd want us all to bear the same last name. We're the Toussaint men, and you should be proud of that."

I looked away.

"If Camille forgives you, is that the end of your diamond business?"

"Unfortunately." I looked at my father again.

"She asked you to sacrifice it."

"No...but I won't repeat your mistakes." I wouldn't put my woman in danger—ever. "I'll find another business, a moral one, something above the table, something that involves paying taxes."

He stared at me across the table, his fingertips on the stem of his glass. "Good for you, Cauldron."

I'd expected him to admonish me, so this was a surprise.

"The time I had with your mother...was the best in my life. Then she gave me a son, a son whom I loved more than anything else in the world. Our time together as a family was brief, but it was wonderful. I'm happy for you. And I'm happy you've learned from my mistakes."

I held my head high and moved on. I took care of my kids, ran the house, did it all with a smile on my face.

But I was dead inside.

I hadn't talked to Jerome about a new client. I had enough money that missing a couple paydays wouldn't be a big deal. When I was this heartbroken, I couldn't put up a good front anyway. Some man would pay a fortune for my time—and he would be deeply disappointed.

As I expected, Grave didn't contact me.

He ripped my heart out and walked away...like it was nothing.

If I'd just kept my mouth shut, he would still be mine.

I'd had the perfect man, and I could have had him so much longer if I'd just bottled all those pretty feelings inside. If I'd just ignored the elephant in the room instead of throwing it in his face. A part of me regretted my actions, but another part of me knew this was inevitable. My feelings became too heavy. My love too complicated. If I went down this road any further, it would just hurt more in the end.

Even though it was hard to believe it could hurt any more than this...

When a week came and went without a text or call, I suspected I would never hear from him again.

He didn't even check on me.

But I told myself it was better this way. If we spoke, the process would start all over. It would be like picking at a scab that had just healed. My best therapy was staying so busy I didn't have time to think about him. That meant taking my kids out after school, hitting the gym morning and night, making sure I didn't have a spare minute to wonder what Grave was doing.

Who he was fucking.

But when I lay in bed to fall asleep, that was when the loneliness hit me—and the longing. I pictured his face so clearly, it was like he was right in front of me. Those chocolate-colored eyes. That enormous physique. The way he smiled only slightly. His deep voice and the way it rumbled inside his chest. He was a real man, and I would never find one like that again.

I started to cry...again.

"God, I'm so pathetic..." I sniffled and wiped away the tears. Then my phone vibrated on the nightstand, and the glow lit up my dark bedroom.

I went still. My heart was like a hammer against my ribs. The adrenaline was fierce. No one texted me this late at night.

No one except him.

I reached for the phone and looked at the message.

How are you? I heard his voice in my head as I read it, deep and powerful, with a hint of sincerity.

I read those three words a dozen more times.

I didn't type back. What was I supposed to say? *I cry every day and I'm utterly miserable? Thanks for asking...* I chose not to say anything at all. It would just refuel a fire that had finally gone out.

If it helps...I'm pretty fucked up.

Moisture built up in my eyes, slowly forming a thin film over my gaze. I didn't blink for a long time because when I did, I'd start to cry again...and I'd just stopped. *Please leave me alone, Grave.* It was hard to send that message, but it was for the best.

He didn't text me again.

I returned from the grocery store and carried all the bags into the house. They were full of snacks and drinks for the kids, string cheese and frozen peanut butter and jelly sandwiches. Cabinets opened and closed, the refrigerator beeping because I left it wide open. So absorbed in what I was doing, I gave a jump when I heard a knock on the door. "Jesus..." With my hand over my heart, I walked across the living room and into the foyer. I had one of those doors made of frosted glass, so I could see the outline of someone on the other side. It was a man—a big man.

Frozen on the spot, I stared at his outline, the color of his maroon shirt, his impressive height. Then I started to smell pine and body soap...sweat and sex in the sheets. Flashbacks hit me unexpectedly, and I shuffled through all of them as I stood there.

"Gonna let me in?"

I took a breath before I opened the door. It was the first time I'd seen him in a week. Mocha-brown eyes. A hard jawline covered with a shadow. His thick arms stretching the fabric of his shirt. His hands were in his pockets, and he stood out in the cold January day, small clouds of vapor coming from his nose.

Paralyzed, all I could do was stare.

My eyes drank him in. I did the same.

After what felt like an eternity, he moved toward me. "Can we talk inside?" He knew I was alone. Had watched my apartment, made sure the kids were dropped off at school and the nanny was elsewhere.

I nodded then stepped aside.

I shut the door and sealed the cold air outside.

He walked into the living room then pulled his hands from his pockets. His eyes fixed on me, and now that we were in private, his stare was intense. It was the look he used to give me when I walked in the door, just seconds before he ravished me against the closest wall he could find.

I wasn't wearing makeup and my hair was thrown in a bun, but he looked at me like I was a stripper about to hit the pole. The longer he stared, the more self-conscious I became. My arms locked over my chest, and I averted my gaze. To stare at this powerful man and know he would never be mine...it was so hard. "I hope you have something important to say...to torture me like this."

"I'm not trying to torture you."

My eyes returned to his. "I'm doing everything I possibly can to move on. I stay busy so I don't think of you, and when I do think of you, I force myself to think about something else. I don't call, I don't text, because it's just too hard. So, if you're here to do anything other than tell me you love me and you want to try...then you're a fucking asshole."

He dropped his chin, like those words had enough punch to make him sick.

That was my answer. "This is so fucked up."

He raised his chin and drew close. "I didn't like the way we left things—"

"And you think we're gonna end things better this time?" My voice went from a whisper to an explosion because he'd barged back into my life just to make me miserable. "What the fuck is wrong with you?"

"I said some harsh things—"

"That you meant. It's fine, Grave. You spoke your truth, and I accept that truth. Now get the fuck out of here—and don't come back." I couldn't believe the audacity, to come back here when he knew how heart-broken I was. "I'm not sorry for breaking our rules. I'm not sorry for telling you I love you. I wish I'd done it sooner and got out quicker."

He closed his eyes for a moment.

"What do you want?" I whispered.

"You aren't the only one who's devastated—"

"Fuck you." I turned away, getting some distance between us, getting that goddamn smell out of my nose. "Get out of my house."

"I mean it—"

"If you meant it, we would be together right now. You'd be on your fucking knees, begging me to take you back." I kept my back to him. "But you're here because...you didn't like *the way we ended things*." I rolled my eyes, holding on to my anger so it would keep the tears at bay.

"I don't want to end up like my brother."

It was such an unexpected thing to say that I turned to look at him, unsure what that meant or why he'd said it.

"I know how he feels about Camille, but he's fucked her over too many times. Maybe they'll work it out, but it'll probably never be the same. That trust is irrevocably broken. I don't want to end up like that...with you."

My arms tightened over my chest, and I tried to read his features like words. "What does that mean?"

A long, hard stare ensued. He studied my face with shifting eyes, considering the words that formed in his head before he said them. "I only do monogamy if I'm in love—and I'm in love with you."

My fingers dug into my arms, letting those words bounce off my invisible armor. He may have said the words I wanted to hear, but that didn't mean he would give me what I wanted. "If that were true, you wouldn't have dumped me."

"My feelings don't change our situation. You're a single mother to two kids, and I'm not looking to be a stepfather. Saying it back wouldn't have helped the situation. Saying it first...wouldn't have helped either."

"Then what's the point of saying it now?"

He gave a slight shake of his head. "I couldn't let you think I didn't love you. Couldn't let you think that our time together meant nothing to me. Didn't want you to think I'd just moved on without a second thought. I sleep alone every night and think of you."

"If that's true, why can't we make this work?"

He looked down at the floor for a while. "It gets complicated the second kids are involved. Honestly, would you even want me around them? Camille was just kidnapped because of me. You know how I earn my money. What kind of mother would ever want an asshole like me near her children?" His eyes narrowed on my face, full of accusation.

"There's a lot more to you than that..."

"An association with me is dangerous, Elise."

"Then walk away. Leave it all behind."

He released a deep breath, his nostrils flaring. "My life's work?"

"It's just work, Grave. I don't know how much money you have, but I don't think you need that either."

"I don't know shit about kids..."

"You think I do?" I asked with a painful laugh. "It's the hardest job I've ever had. Every time they hit a new age, I have to head back to the drawing board and start over. You just do the best you can and love them along the way."

He looked away again.

"Grave, I never asked you to be their stepfather. I never asked you for anything. I just wanted you to know how I feel about you...because I couldn't keep it in any longer. We can be together in private, like we've been doing this entire time. Nothing needs to change. I just want to be able to say how I feel when I feel it."

"But it does need to change." He looked at me again. "Because I want to have this experience with someone and not step into the middle of it. I want it from the beginning. I want to be there when my child is born. I want to take care of them in the middle of the night when you're too tired. I want someone to carry on my name when I'm gone. I can't wait ten years to start that process, so there is no other option."

"But we don't need to do that right this second. Whenever you're ready."

"Like I already said, I don't want to be a stepfather."

"Then don't be a stepfather," I said. "You can be their friend. Nothing wrong with that."

He held my gaze and took a deep breath.

"Even if I didn't already have kids, you'd have to give up everything anyway. Because I'm not having your babies if you're still living that life. They'd need to be safe, and your retirement is the only way to ensure that. Whether it's with me or Camille...or someone else...you'd have to step away, regardless."

He averted his gaze and remained quiet for a long time. "I don't know how I got here. Last week, we were just having fun, and now...I have to make a decision."

"The decision doesn't need to be made now."

"But it does." His eyes lifted to me. "Because if we continue this relationship, it's not the same. It's not a man and his whore. It's a man with his woman. And as your man, I need to protect not only you, but those you care about. That means...my life needs to change. I can't risk someone taking you to hurt me...or taking someone else."

I couldn't even allow myself to think about it.

"So yes, the decision needs to be made, and it needs to be made today."

"So...we're either in this for the long haul...or we aren't together at all?"

"Yes."

I prayed it was the first one.

He moved for the door. "I'll let you know."

I watched him walk away, knowing I couldn't interfere with his decision. I wouldn't want him to be with me because I convinced him. I wanted him to be with me because that's what he wanted. I wanted him to give up everything for me—because he wanted me that badly.

32

CAMILLE

Cauldron sat across from me in the restaurant, his shoulders broad in the blazer he wore. The waitress was a fine piece of ass, but he didn't seem to notice because his eyes were glued to me the entire time.

With the exception of his phone.

It seemed to be vibrating in his pocket a lot because he glanced at it repeatedly but never responded to the person trying to talk to him.

"You can get that—"

"It's fine."

The waitress brought our entrees, and we ate in near silence. After being apart for so long, it seemed like we should have a lot to say, but there was nothing new to talk about. We already knew each other. Knew what we wanted out of life. We were stuck in this limbo because of me, when we could be in the dining room downstairs, his butler attending to our every whim.

"How's work?" I asked.

"I sold the business."

"*You what?*" I nearly dropped my fork.

He kept his cool composure. "I sold it for far more than it's worth, so I'm happy with the deal."

"But that was...sudden."

"I meant everything I said to you. I'm all in."

"Cauldron, I never asked you to do that—"

"I've learned from my father's mistakes. I've learned from my own mistakes. Whenever you're ready to come home with me, our lives will be different. We'll occupy the master as man and woman, and then eventually, man and wife. My home will be your home. And then one day...that home will be shared with little people who share our likeness. Whenever you're ready for it."

I knew he was tempting me, making me an offer I couldn't refuse. I could leave my apartment and return to the estate where I'd fallen in love. Our future had everything I wanted. All I had to do was pack my bags and leave.

His eyes watched my expression, strained for a reaction.

"That—that sounds nice. What will you do now? Business-wise?"

"I have a few ideas."

"Like?"

"The restaurant business. Maybe the wine business. Or maybe even the luxury hotel business."

I gave a slight nod. "Those all sound like good ideas."

"I love food, wine, and luxury, so it makes sense. I don't love paying taxes...but that's how it goes."

I gave a slight smile. "I'd love to help you...if you're willing."

His eyes took in my face. "I'd love that."

After a moment, his phone started to vibrate again. I could hear it in his pocket.

"Cauldron, who's trying to get a hold of you?"

He released a sigh of irritation. "Grave is blowing up my phone. I'll deal with him after dinner."

"Maybe it's important."

"He can wait."

"Cauldron, it's fine, really."

He gave another sigh before he reached for his phone to read the messages. But before he could, it started to ring. Cauldron answered. "Can we talk later? I'm at dinner with Camille. At Le Livia. Why?" He gave an irritated sigh then hung up.

"I'm guessing Grave is joining us."

"Yes." He stuffed his phone into the pocket inside his jacket. "I'm sorry."

"It's fine. Must be important."

"Not so important that it can't wait." He took a few bites of his food, but his appetite seemed to have been extinguished.

"I have to get going soon anyway..."

He stiffened slightly but didn't question me.

"Bartholomew wants me to help him with something."

Cauldron didn't say a word. Probably because he knew he would scream if he did.

"How will that work?" I asked. "You know, if I moved back home…"

He was quiet for a long time, like he needed time to resolve his anger. "If he gives you a day's notice, you could always take my plane to Paris. I could accompany you as well."

"Did he say how long he needs me?"

His eyes looked enraged. "No."

I could see this was killing him. "I'll talk to him and see if we can work something out."

Cauldron said nothing more on the subject, like he just wanted to drop it.

A couple minutes later, Grave entered the restaurant and carried his own chair to our table.

"What the fuck are you doing?" Cauldron said in a quiet voice.

"I said I need to talk to you."

"And this can't wait thirty minutes?" Cauldron snapped.

"I thought it would be better to talk to you both anyway."

"Oh good," Cauldron said. "Why don't you have some of my steak, then?"

Grave drew the plate toward himself and took a bite.

Cauldron shook his head. "Such a jackass."

Brothers.

"I saw Elise today," Grave said. "Stopped by her place."

"Why?" I asked, knowing it must have been torture for her.

"Why?" Grave asked. "I thought that would be obvious..."

"Nothing is obvious when it comes to you, Grave," Cauldron said.

"I told her I didn't want to fuck up my life the way Cauldron has."

"Thanks," Cauldron said coldly.

Grave ignored him. "I told her I loved her."

I smiled. "That's great."

"You needed to ruin our dinner to tell us that?" Cauldron asked incredulously. "Because you told a woman you loved her?"

Grave turned to him. "Am I cockblocking you or something? You weren't going to get laid anyway."

I slid my foot up Cauldron's pant leg. "Actually, he was..."

Both men turned to me.

"And still is," I said. "Don't worry."

A slight smile moved on to Cauldron's lips. Now he looked like a different man, relaxing in his chair, bringing the wine to his mouth for a drink. "The floor is yours, Grave."

Grave looked at me again. "I want to be with her, but I have to walk away from everything before I do. It's a hard decision. It's been my entire life. Not sure who I would be without it."

"You accept her children, then?" I asked.

"She said we don't need to rush into that," he said. "And she said I didn't need to be a stepfather if I didn't want to. Could be their friend instead."

"That sounds nice," I said.

"I can't be in a relationship with her when I have the constant threat of doom hanging over my head. It's not just her safety I'm worried about. It's her kids, too. I'd kill myself if something happened to any of them." Grave looked at neither of us as he spoke, almost talking to himself.

"This doesn't sound like a dilemma," Cauldron said. "You already know what you want to do—but you don't want to do it."

Grave sank into his chair and looked at his brother. "I suppose."

"It's not that bad." Now it seemed like I wasn't there. It was just the two of them talking. "I sold the business this morning. I got far more than the asking price. It's hard to walk away from that part of your identity—but it's worth it." His eyes flicked to me and lingered for a moment.

I felt the warmth melt inside me.

"There's more to life than work," Cauldron said. "And there are things far more rewarding than money—like a good woman."

Grave was quiet for a while, and then he gave a nod. "You're right."

"Go for it." Cauldron clapped his brother on the shoulder. "I wonder what Father will think."

"He won't be angry," Grave said.

"You think?" Cauldron asked.

He grabbed Cauldron's wineglass and took a drink. "Not when I tell him grandkids are on the way."

When I opened the door, I came face-to-face with Bartholomew.

Fashioned in a black jacket and his boots, he looked like he was born in darkness. Thrived in darkness. His hair was such a deep color that women could only attain it by dyeing theirs midnight black. His intelligent eyes locked on my face, having an entire conversation in silence.

"Just let me get my coat." I grabbed it from the rack, and we walked out.

Instead of having a driver take us where we needed to go, he was the one behind the wheel.

The silence became so heavy that I needed to break it. "How are you?"

"How am I?" He drove with one hand on the wheel, the roads slick from the afternoon rain. "No one's ever asked me that before."

"There's a first time for everything, right?"

He pulled over to the side of the road. On the opposite side, there was some kind of gathering going on. Everyone wore black, so I assumed it was a funeral or mass.

"Did you lose someone?"

"I have no one to lose." He looked out the window for a long time before he turned back to me. "There's someone I need to speak to. Your job is to distract the woman he's brought. Pretty routine."

"Alright. But do you think this is appropriate at a funeral?"

He cracked a slight smile before he opened the door. "You think I care what's appropriate?"

An hour later, he drove me back to my apartment.

"I hear Cauldron sold the business." He put the car in park and killed the engine. It was warm inside, but after a couple minutes, that would change.

"I hear the same."

"Did you ask him to?"

"No. It was his decision."

"What will he do now?"

"He has a couple business plans in mind..."

"Legal, legitimate businesses?"

"Yes."

He gave a slow nod. "Snooze-fest."

"Maybe one day you'll fall in love and do the same."

He gave me a steady stare, his eyes hard but his mouth slightly playful. "Right."

I stared at him for a while, regarding him as a friend but feeling like he was a stranger at the same time. "I think I'm going back to Cap-Ferrat..."

There was a subtle change to his eyes, his brows lowering over his face. "Cauldron and I have a deal."

"I'll still come here when you need me. I just need a day's notice. Cauldron said I could take his plane."

He stared at me for a while, letting the silence flow over us in waves. "I know what you're doing."

"What am I doing?" I asked, my bewilderment sincere.

"You're trying to make me feel bad. But I've never felt bad about anything I've ever said or done."

"That's not what I was trying to do."

"Then you won't be disappointed when I tell you the deal is still on. That was my price."

"And it was a fair price."

He continued to study me.

"How long is this deal going to last, exactly?"

"Why?"

"I hope to be a wife and a mother in a couple years. Can't take off to Paris for a few days with my babies at home."

"Cauldron can't take care of them?" he asked incredulously.

"If they're too young, I think he'd lose his mind."

He gave a quiet laugh. "How about a year? That seem fair?"

"I can do a year."

"Alright." He extended his hand to me.

We shook on it.

"But what will you do when the year is over?" I asked.

Bartholomew looked out the windshield again. "I guess I'll have to find someone else... Wish me luck."

"A lot of women would kill for this job. It's exciting."

"But few can handle it. They lack the professional sternness I require."

"I see..."

"You've been in the game long enough to know how all this works. Most haven't."

"Well, Cauldron will be happy to know there's an expiration date."

"He'd be happier to know that I got shot on the job," he said with a mild laugh.

"He likes you."

"But he doesn't like that I spend time with you. He's one of those..."

"One of those what?"

"Jealous lovers." He looked at me head on. "Are you one of those too?"

If Cauldron spent time alone with a beautiful woman, it'd drive me insane. "Yes."

"Then you're perfect for each other." He opened the door and got out.

I walked with him to the front door. "You don't have to walk me every time."

"I know." He waited for me to open the front door, hands in his pockets, his eyes wide awake when mine were growing tired.

"Goodnight."

"Goodnight, Camille." After the door was shut, he walked back to his car and drove off.

I'd just finished loading the dishwasher and cleaning up the kitchen when the front door opened and closed. Heavy footsteps were loud against the hardwood floor, the person announcing their presence rather than masking it.

I wasn't scared. I knew exactly who it was.

Cauldron entered the kitchen, in a long-sleeved shirt and jeans, changed out of his dinner clothes. The fact that he just walked in told me he'd been watching the apartment. He'd watched Bartholomew drop me off then made his move once I was alone.

"What are you doing here?" I asked as I dried my hands with the towel. "It's almost midnight."

He strode toward me slowly, his eyes taking in my face. "You said I was going to get laid tonight." He stopped when he was directly in front of me, his lips just inches from mine.

"Did I?" I eyed his mouth, my skin turning warm with goose bumps.

"Don't tease me, baby." He moved again, guiding me back to the kitchen counter, pinning me in place with his hands on either side of me.

As he towered over me, my hands started at his biceps and slowly moved up, gripping the large muscles of his shoulders. My arms hooked around his neck, anchoring him to me in the dim kitchen light.

His hands went to my waist, and his fingers dug into my hips and a bit into my ass. He pushed into me harder then dropped his mouth to mine, sealing my lips with his masculine kiss. It was rough and hungry, taking the lead, like he wanted everything he could take. He kissed me then squeezed me, bringing my stomach right against his hard erection in his jeans. It was more than passionate, more than lustful. It was desperate.

He lifted me onto the counter then stood between my thighs, kissing me as he gripped my ass through my jeans.

My hand cupped his face, my fingers digging into his hair. My apartment had been silent, but now it was full of our feverish kisses, our elevated breaths as we clung to each other.

He suddenly whisked me away, holding me against his body as he carried me all the way up the stairs to my bedroom, kissing me at the same time, squeezing my ass with those big hands.

He dropped me on the bed and tugged his shirt over his head. A hard, chiseled body appeared, his physicality so damn sexy. The jeans came next and then the boxers underneath. He stood in front of the bed in all his glory, ripped with muscle, his aching cock ready to plow into me.

His knees hit the bed, and he yanked my clothes off, starting with my jeans. He tugged them off in one fluid motion then got my thong off next. I sat up so I could get my shirt off, but he tugged at my hips then pressed his face between my legs.

"Oh..." I hadn't expected it, and the second I felt his kiss, I was paralyzed. It started off as a slow kiss, a gentle spin of his sexy tongue. And then the pressure built gradually, growing in intensity until I was writhing with my hand cupping the back of his head, pulling him harder into me. "Yes..." I came with tears in my eyes, grinding my heat right into his mouth.

His mouth left my sex, and he climbed up my body.

I couldn't see clearly, not when the tears blurred my vision.

His thumb caught a tear, and then he kissed me hard, sliding his tongue into my mouth so I could taste him. He pushed inside me in a single thrust, his cock harder than it'd ever been, and delved deep inside me until it hurt.

I moaned into his mouth as my nails sliced him.

He tilted my hips and pinned one knee with his arm. Then he thrust into me hard and quick, so turned on, he needed his release as quickly as possible. We bounced together on the bed, grunting and moaning, our bodies so slick and tight.

"Cauldron..." I grabbed on to his ass and tugged him into me.

The sound of his name was his threshold, and he came with an animal-like groan. His jaw went tight. His skin darkened with a tint of red. He dumped himself inside me, filling me with a load that would keep me warm all night long.

Feeling him inside me made me hot all over again. My body continued to latch on to his because I didn't want to let him go. I wanted it to continue. "Don't stop..."

Those words either invigorated him, or he was so charged that he wasn't going to deflate anyway because he was rock hard and still pumping inside me, sliding through our come, pounding me into the bed like he was going to break it.

"Yes..." My nails clawed down his back as I felt the heat fill my center. It built up quickly then exploded, my eyes wet once more. It felt so good, so raw, as if I hadn't just exploded minutes ago. It was brand-new.

He followed quickly afterward, the two of us getting off several times in just a few minutes. We were like animals desperate to devour each other. We were fire and gasoline, igniting together and consuming us both.

When I opened my eyes, it was morning.

Sunlight poured through the window because I'd forgotten to close the curtain. My hand automatically reached for the man beside me, but all I felt were cold sheets. I turned abruptly to where he should be—and felt ice splash on my face.

He was gone.

I looked at his nightstand for his keys and wallet, but there was nothing there. His clothes weren't on the floor either.

Did he really just fuck me and leave?

I turned to get out of bed when I spotted the flower on my nightstand. A pink rose. There was a handwritten letter.

Baby,

I wanted to watch you sleep, but I know how hungry you get in the morning. See you downstairs.

When I set down the note, I heard the movements of pots and pans. All the dismay left my body, and a smile replaced it. I pulled on sweatpants and a crop top and headed downstairs, finding Cauldron working in the kitchen in the clothes he'd worn the night before.

"What's that smell?"

"Bacon, eggs, and pancakes." He set the dirty pan in the sink. "At least, that's what I hope you smell." He turned to me, his hair messy from the night before, his handsome smile bright like the morning sunshine. "Good morning." He hugged me close and kissed me.

"Morning..." I felt my cheeks warm.

He got back to work, scooping the pancakes onto the plate, along with the eggs and bacon, before handing it to me. "I'll get your coffee."

I looked at the food, which was still steaming. "Where did you learn this?"

He filled my mug then added the cream, remembering how I took my coffee. When he set it on the table, he had a knowing grin on his face. "I didn't always have a butler."

We sat together at the dining table, eating one of the best breakfasts I'd ever had.

"You know, I prefer your cooking to your chefs'," I said.

"Yeah?" he asked. "Looks like I've found a new job as a cook."

We fell into comfortable silence, the two of us enjoying our breakfast on this cold winter day.

"So, I was thinking..." I slid my piece of pancake into the syrup before placing it in my mouth. "I should move back home with you."

He paused as he looked at me, happiness written all over his face. "Wow, I didn't realize the breakfast was *that* good."

I chuckled with my mouth closed, another bite of food between my teeth.

"You have no idea how happy that makes me."

"I told Bartholomew I could come back whenever he needs me. He said he wants a year of service."

Cauldron dropped his look at the topic. "He's a stickler, isn't he?"

"I think it's a fair trade for what he did."

"Can't argue with that..."

"I think I'll keep my apartment. That way, I have a place to go whenever I'm in town."

"Why wouldn't we stay at my place?" he asked. "It's safer. There's an entire staff waiting for us."

"But what about when I come alone?"

"I doubt you'll come alone, and if you do, that apartment is still yours. You're the woman of the house. You could sell this place and give the money back to Grave."

"That's true..." It would be nice to return his money.

"We can figure it out later," he said. "Right now...I'm just happy."

33

GRAVE

I waited outside her apartment.

The nanny pulled out of the parking garage with the kids in the back seat, taking them to school in the morning. When the coast was clear, I walked right up to her front door and knocked.

I didn't give her any warning. Just showed up.

She opened the door a moment later in her athleisure attire, like she was about to head to the gym for her daily workout. In tight leggings and a white sports bra, she was a fit chick with a sexy booty.

Her eyes were guarded as she looked at me, as if she anticipated the answer she didn't want.

We stared at each other for a while.

"Can I come in?" I finally asked.

My voice seemed to snap her out of her focus. "Sure."

We entered her living room, pictures of her and her kids everywhere. It was a home. It gave me a jolt of unease, but I'd already made my decision, and there was no going back. I faced her, seeing her fear linger in her eyes. Her arms moved across her chest, her usual posture when she was putting on a front.

"I want this."

She tried to keep up her front, but slowly, she started to melt. "Yeah?"

"Yeah."

She took a slow breath, a film moving over her eyes.

"I'll sell the business. Live a quiet life. But I don't want to rush into anything."

"I never asked you to."

"Someday...when I'm ready...I'll meet them."

She nodded. "That's fine with me, Grave."

"Your kids will be out of the house in less than ten years. Are you sure this is something you'd want to start over?"

"What do you mean?"

"Having a couple babies. I know raising a family is hard. You did it once. Now you'll have to do it again."

"Hard?" she asked, a slight smile on her lips. "It wouldn't be nearly as enjoyable if it were easy. The hardness is the best part. I would absolutely do it again, especially with you. No problem there."

I pictured her pregnant with my kid, her feet swollen, me taking care of her so she wouldn't have to waddle around the house. I pictured us living at my estate outside Paris, enough room for four kids, thousands of acres for them to enjoy. It was a life I'd pictured with Camille, but now this picture looked better, looked more vibrant. "Are you free tonight?"

"Tonight?" she asked, her eyebrow cocked. "I'm free right now."

I released a quiet chuckle, seeing her undress me with those demanding eyes. "Yeah?"

"Yeah."

I walked toward her, my hands touching her for the first time, planting around her waist with my thumbs over her belly. Her long hair was pulled back in a tight band, showing the feminine contours of her face. I dipped my head down as I came close to her, landing with the softness of a pillow.

It felt like a year since I'd last kissed her, even though it'd just been a week. And this kiss was sweeter because it was everlasting and because she was the last woman I would ever kiss. My hands reached for her ass, and I lifted her to me so I wouldn't have to bend my neck to kiss her far below. Her legs wrapped around my waist, and I kissed her as I held on to her juicy ass.

Her arms hooked around my neck, and she expressed all her emotions through her kiss. Her job was supposed to be to satisfy me, but then she took it a step further by making me feel like a man, making me feel like the only man she'd ever set her eyes on. She wasn't afraid to wear her heart on her sleeve, to be transparent in her feelings, to love me without actually saying it.

I carried her to her bedroom and dropped her onto the bed.

Her hands yanked my sweater over my head before she planted her palms against my hard chest. Her lips were on me again, not wanting to break our kiss for more than a second.

I tugged off her leggings, taking her sneakers with them.

Her hands popped the button on my jeans.

We were naked together except for the sports bra, and I sank into her like a man claiming undiscovered land. I buried my entire length inside her and ignored the small wince she made.

It felt so good to be inside her again.

Her legs locked around my waist again, and we moved together, clawing at each other as we fucked. My hand fisted her hair, and I breathed into her cheek. "Fuck... this pussy." It was already indescribable to fuck a woman you desired, but it was another level to fuck a woman you couldn't live without, a woman you would give up everything for. And when I felt how wet she was, felt how much she wanted me, there were no words. "I love you." I said it as I nailed her, said it as I fucked her like a whore.

She dug her nails harder into me, meeting my thrusts with deep pants. "I love you too."

I walked in the door of Camille's apartment. There were a couple suitcases in the entryway. "Camille?"

She came down the stairs a moment later, wearing leggings and a sweater like she was doing housework.

"Hey."

"Going on a trip?"

"Kinda. A very long trip." She wiped the sweat from her forehead with the back of her palm. "Cauldron and I are going back to Cap-Ferrat...back home."

"That's great news." I was happy for my brother. He finally got what he wanted—and he was mature enough not to fuck it up again. "Are you selling the place?"

"You're selling the place. It's yours."

"It was a gift, Camille."

"I know, and while I appreciate that, I don't need it. It would be wrong to keep your money, Grave. I have Cauldron for what I need."

I gave a slight nod.

"You can sell it furnished. I have nowhere to put this stuff."

"Do you guys ever think about living in Paris full time?"

She shrugged. "I think Cauldron likes the weather and his yacht. Why?"

I looked around at her apartment. "It's been nice having my brother around…"

Her eyes softened slightly. "We'll always visit, Grave. You can always come to us…Elise too."

She'd probably like a vacation like that.

Camille studied my features. "There is an Elise, yes?"

"I talked to her."

"And…?"

"And what? I told you I would make it work."

"That's great. She must have been so happy."

She'd fucked my brains out, so yes, she was ecstatic.

"I'm happy for you."

"I'm happy for you too." When I looked at her, my eyes dipped down to her necklace then quickly looked away. Our former lives felt so long ago they didn't feel real anymore, almost folklore. "Need help with anything?"

"Cauldron should be here any minute to collect everything."

"So you're leaving today, then?"

"Yep. It'll be nice to be home."

A few minutes later, Cauldron walked inside. His men entered and gathered all the suitcases that held her possessions. Cauldron walked up to me and patted me on the arm. "How'd it go with Elise?"

"I'm exhausted. Does that answer your question?"

Cauldron grinned before he clapped me on the shoulder. "What's next?"

"Selling the business. Telling Father. Finding something else to do with my time."

"Same here."

"I'm a bit bummed you'll be in Cap-Ferrat," I said. "It was nice having you down the street."

My brother stared at me for a long time, like he struggled to find the words. "You know you're always welcome, Grave. Elise and her kids too—whenever you're ready for that. Camille has to come back for Bartholomew regularly, so we'll be popping in."

I nodded. "Sounds good."

He stared.

I stared back. "I'm glad we're brothers again."

His expression remained rigid, but there was a slight hitch in his breathing. "Yeah...me too."

34

CAMILLE

We passed through the gates then entered the roundabout.

The house came into view, the water fountain with lily pads in the center. The tall oak trees cast shade across the pavers in the driveway. The colorful flowers were extinguished by winter's bite, but it was still a beautiful day.

Hugo stood out front, ready to receive us.

I still remembered the morning I'd left, head held high with tears bottled deep. It made my heart sink in sadness because that wound would always be fresh, regardless of the passage of time.

We left the car and walked to the front door.

Hugo gave me a slight bow. "It's nice to have you back, Camille. Didn't feel the same without you."

I gave him a smile. "That's nice of you to say."

"And it's especially nice because I mean it."

I reached for his arm and gave him a squeeze. "It's great to be back." I entered the foyer, the smell of the hardwood and fresh flowers immediate. It was like walking back in time, all the times I walked through here to Cauldron's study.

The men brought the luggage inside, carrying everything up the long staircase to the top floor.

Cauldron stepped inside, sliding his sunglasses into the neckline of his shirt. "Six more weeks until spring. Then it'll really feel like home."

"It already does," I said, looking at him.

His arm circled my waist, and he dipped his head to kiss me.

"It's a fairly warm day," Hugo said. "Would you like to have lunch on the terrace?"

"That sounds great, Hugo." Cauldron moved to the staircase. After the staff returned from their drop-off, he gestured for me to go first.

I took the long journey up the stairs to the third floor then entered his bedroom. I meant, our bedroom. It was exactly as I remembered it, spacious and elegant, with its own living room and private patio with a view of the water. My suitcases were placed in the closet, where half of it was empty so I could hang up all my things.

Cauldron remained in the doorway, watching me walk around.

"What?" I asked when his stare continued.

He didn't answer.

I walked into the closet and looked around. I hated unpacking, so I chose to be lazy and leave the bags there before I exited again.

He didn't move.

"Seriously, why do you keep staring at me?"

His arms crossed over his chest as he leaned against the doorframe. "Just want to see you make yourself at home."

It was an odd explanation, and I didn't buy it. When I turned to admire the flowers on the nightstand, I noticed the colorful reflection of a diamond. The sunlight came through the open windows and made it shine so brilliantly. When I got closer, I realized it wasn't a bracelet or earrings.

But a ring.

A single, cut diamond in a platinum band. It was a beautiful rock, a princess cut, absolutely gorgeous.

I took a breath then looked at him.

He remained by the door, watching me. "It's yours whenever you want it."

Still in disbelief, I stared. "You made it sound like marriage was for some time in the future—"

"I didn't want to ask you to marry me to get you back. I didn't want to use it as a bandage for our problems. Unless I earned you back on my own, I didn't deserve to ask you to be my wife. But now that you're home... fair game."

I picked up the ring off the nightstand. "You didn't have to do this, Cauldron. I never needed a proposal from you. I just wanted—"

"A commitment." He came around the bed, coming closer to me. "I know. But I want more than that. I'm asking you because I want us together forever, every day, the two of us. So please stop torturing me and say yes."

"Cauldron..."

"Or spare me by saying nothing at all...and put it on whenever you're ready."

My eyes shifted back and forth between his, seeing the way he turned guarded in preparation for rejection. "Cauldron...you know my answer is yes."

His eyes released their suspense and relaxed. "Then put it on." He grabbed my hand and guided the diamond ring onto my finger. It was a perfect fit because my jeweler fiancé knew my exact size.

It looked even more beautiful on my finger. With every subtle turn of my hand, I watched it sparkle. I watched our eternal love dance across my eyes. "It's beautiful..."

"I sold off everything else but this—because I wanted it to be yours. I won't bore you with the details of this diamond, but I can tell you there's no better one in this world, none with this clarity."

"Honestly, you could have given me a ring with a button glued to it and I still would have loved it."

He smiled. "If only I'd known beforehand...would have saved me a lot of money."

I chuckled, enjoying the break in tension that had my muscles so tight. Cauldron had just asked me to marry him...and I said yes. I could have chosen not to forgive him. I could have said it would never work between us. Could have moved on with my life. Might have found someone else. Might have slept with Bartholomew. But I never would have been as happy as I was now—and that was how I knew I'd made the right decision. "When should we get married?"

His eyes lit up brighter than they ever had, glowing like the summer sunset. "How about in the spring?"

EPILOGUE
CAULDRON

It was a beautiful spring day, the temperature moderate but hinting at the impending summer. Flowers were in bloom across the property, red geraniums and white lilies. The lawn had been perfectly manicured for our wedding, and the ocean breeze made it all the way up the cliff.

Grave clapped me on the shoulder. "You look nervous."

I looked at him, seeing him wear a teasing smile. "You look like shit."

"Really?" He glanced past me to where Elise sat in her dress. "Because I woke up with Elise on my dick, so I don't think that's true."

"She just has bad taste."

"Well, she tastes pretty good to me..."

I rolled my eyes. "TMI."

We were like kids again, teasing each other for every little thing. He stood beside me in his suit, ready to hand me the rings when my bride left the house. It was a small wedding, just a dozen people, including my father.

The violinist started to play.

"Showtime," Grave said. "Hopefully she shows up..."

"I will punch you on my wedding day."

"And I'll punch you right back."

I took a deep breath when I saw the back doors open. It was hard to see her because of all the trees in the way, but I caught glimpses of her white gown. She eventually made it down the path, curving around the trees until she came into view.

On my father's arm, she looked more beautiful than I'd ever seen her.

Long, blond hair in beautiful curls, her eyes bright like the sunshine, and the diamonds I gave her making her sparkle. Her gown trailed behind her, and she held the bouquet of white flowers to her chest as she drew near.

Her eyes landed on mine.

Mine locked on hers.

The rest was like a dream.

She floated to me like a cloud, and before I could take a breath, she was in front of me, my father placing her hand in mine.

I clasped it, feeling its softness in mine. I faced her, seeing the most beautiful woman I'd ever laid eyes on. She was mine to cherish. Mine to hold. Mine to love as long as I lived. Our love started on a yacht with threats of violence, but it ended with a story from an entirely different book.

I could hardly focus on anything that was said, so enraptured by the way she looked at me, like she loved me despite my flaws and loved me for me, not my money. When my time passed and our bodies aged, she would still be there. I could lose everything tomorrow, and she'd be sitting on the street corner beside me.

It was unconditional.

On that spring day, I promised to love her forever, and she promised the same to me.

And then I married her.

My next book is all about drug-lord enigma Bartholomew...and how he falls for the daughter of the Skull King.

10/10 spice.

Enemies to lovers.

#AlphaAlert

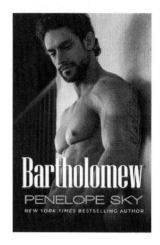

<u>Order Now</u>

Also, I have TWO additional epilogue chapters about Cauldron and Grave. If you'd like to read them, just sign up for my newsletter and you'll get them on November 1! You'll also get a sneak peek of my next book, Bartholomew. **<u>Sign up now!</u>**

Looking for a new author?

My publisher has a brand-new author coming on the scene. Allie Kinsley writes contemporary romance with bad boys who are actually good guys, and heroines that need the right man to come along and put them back together. *Bad Fix* releases on November 1st, so preorder your copy now or read it free in KU!

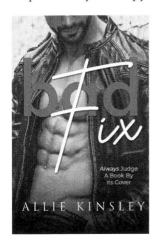

Faith:

I used to be a good girl—believe it or not. Used to bend over backward to make my parents proud. Did whatever I could to please my ex. It was all for nothing—because I've hit rock bottom.

Maybe even below rock bottom.

The only way to get away from everyone and everything is to get the hell out of Dodge. So that's what I do. I start over someplace new, someplace big—a needle in a haystack.

A new life in New York requires money, so I walk into a bar and ask for a job.

Adam owns the place. Six-foot-something, with sleeves of tattoos and a panty-dropping smile, he's what I'd call a hunk. In a different time, I would have done anything to make him mine. But that was then...and this is now. He agrees to give me a job, but that look in his eyes tells me he wants to give me more than that.

Too bad I'm done with men. I don't need another man to break me.

I need a man to fix me—and this guy is a bad fix.

Adam:

I hire Faith and stare at her every chance I get. Drop-dead gorgeous but dead behind the eyes. Interesting mix.

I can feel the spark between us like a lightning strike, but she pretends it's not there. My charm and smile wins over every woman I've ever wanted—but not this one. They say people put up walls. Well...Faith puts up skyscrapers. I could save myself time and hassle and move on to someone else...but I don't want to.

Then I realize the truth—she's scared.

Scared that I'll hurt her.

Like all men, I've done things I'm not proud of. Said things I shouldn't have. But I would never do those things to her.

Not when I can see she's already been broken into a million pieces. Not when she's skittish at the slightest touch. Not when she's taken every single measure to be invisible, like shave her head, hide her curves under baggy clothes, doing everything she possibly can to hide how utterly beautiful she is. I'd have to be blind not to see it.

I want to fix her. I want to bring life back to her eyes. A smile to her lips.

But how do I convince her to let me?

Order Now

Made in United States
Orlando, FL
26 April 2025

60799837R00238